*A
Harlequin
Romance*

OTHER
Harlequin Romances
by JOYCE DINGWELL

THE CATTLEMAN

by

JOYCE DINGWELL

HARLEQUIN BOOKS

TORONTO
WINNIPEG

Original hard cover edition published in 1974
by Mills & Boon Limited.

SBN 373-01856-8

Harlequin edition published February 1975

Printed in Canada

CHAPTER ONE

'WHY did your mother name you Robin? There are no robins in Australia. Are you English them? But you have a brown face instead of white, and you don't look like a pommie.'

It all came in one breath, quite an effort for a small boy rendered half his size again by doubling himself over to peer at Robin from the other side of Ribbons' forelegs, Robin being doubled over herself on this side to adjust one of Ribbons' straps.

Robin regarded the boy thoughtfully – tow-haired, fair-skinned, two front teeth missing. Even with the vocal difference that the loss of two teeth must make she pinpointed him as the new English kid next door, next door being some miles away as homesteads went, but at the boundary fence, as both of them were now, only several yards. Robin had ridden out with her twin Jim; the Glenville youngster would have driven, or ridden, with his father. Yes, it had to be young Glenville. Kids don't drop out of the sky.

'Well, if I'm not one,' she retorted, 'you certainly are.' (Because, she grinned, there was no mistaking, even with the missing teeth, that correct tone.)

'You mean a pommie?'

'Yes.'

'A pommie is all right. I've been told so. It means cheeks like pomegranates.' A puzzled pause. 'What are pomegranates?'

'Kind of apples.'

'Well, why couldn't they say so?'

'If they had,' Robin told the child, straightening up from Ribbons, the boy instantly copying her, 'you'd be called Appley.'

'I don't think I'd like that,' he declined, 'the other will do. You didn't say why you were named Robin.'

'How did you know I was?'

'I heard talk.' – 'Heard talk' would be right, Robin mentally conceded. In an outback place like Yarani there were so few people to talk to or talk about that you would 'hear talk'.

'Did your mother like birds?' persisted the boy.

'Flowers. She visited England once and fell in love with the field flowers.'

'I know the rest,' the boy claimed triumphantly. 'She called you after that pink marsh one, she called you Ragsy Robin.'

'*Ragged* Robin, and not quite that, just the Robin bit. But I think she had them in mind.'

'I like it. The Ragsy part, I mean.' The child ignored her correction. 'Can I call you Ragsy?'

'I don't think you'll be calling me anything, we're miles apart.'

'We're not now,' he pointed out.

'I rode out with my brother to see to some fences. You drove out with your father.'

'No.'

'Well, you rode then.'

'No. I mean, he's not my father.'

'Oh, uncle then.'

'Brother,' the child said.

'Don't tell whoppers,' Robin advised; she supplemented her work with Jim running a district school of nine pupils, so knew the language. Also, at this moment she could see their neighbour, if only partially, on the other side of the boundary, partially since he was tinkering around with his jeep, and he was all of thirty and some, she judged, far too advanced to have such a juvenile brother.

'He is, too, my brother,' defended the boy. 'But I don't think he likes it much.'

6

"Why? Are you naughty?"

'I think I'm good, but I've heard him say I'm a basement,' the boy said vaguely.

Robin decided it must be an embarrassment, which to thirty and some a young brother of no more than six or seven certainly could prove. The boy must be the child that the second wife of old Glenville's widowed son-in-law had brought to her marriage. So involved, Robin thought with dislike ... she had dislike for everything Glenville ... none of the Mansfields had gone in for such family intrigue.

Yes, that would be the relationship. Because of boarding school, and, later, a city job, Robin had been away from Yarani for some time, but her mother had always kept her up to date. Firstly, and a long time ago now, old Glenville had died. Later, also, his only child, a daughter, in childbirth. Then, much later again, indeed quite recently, there had been a marriage in England when the widower had visited there ... or so Yarani had 'heard talk'. Robin chewed her lip, trying to remember more about the Glenvilles ... *that is apart from the feud which she always saw to it that she remembered very well.* Too well, her twin always complained.

The feud had been almost two decades ago, but its ashes always had been kept red and hot ... by the Mansfield side, anyhow. 'Briefly,' Robin's mother had sighed of her stubborn father-in-law, 'while surveying for a new road, a Government official discovered that the Mansfields had some of the Glenville property. That it wasn't much use, anyway, didn't rate with your grandfather, and he instantly staged a dreadful row.'

'It takes two,' Robin had said loyally.

'You as well.' Mrs. Mansfield had shaken her head over her daughter.

Jim, the man of the family (after Grandfather, of course), had taken little interest. Like his mother, and his father before him ... but never, *never* Grandfather ... he did not believe in keeping feudal fires red and hot. Grandfather had, so Robin had. She was a 'Me, too,' Jim always had accused; everything that Grandfather Mansfield had said or done, she said and did likewise.

That old Glenville with his extra property ... and a sense of what was to come? ... had got rid of his sheep and gone in for Brahma cattle instead had constituted no outrage at any time for Jim.

'Good luck to him,' he not only had said then, but also said later when wool had lost its boom but cattle had gone up ... while the Mansfields had stuck to sheep.

But Robin, smaller than that child now on the other side of Ribbons when it had first happened, had protested angrily, if not understanding a word, had protested on behalf of Grandfather and the Mansfields. Grandfather Mansfield, she could still recall, had picked her up and said: 'That's my girl.'

After a while he had added: 'Only one thing is wrong, Rob.' He had sighed. 'One day you'll marry and not be a Mansfield. However' ... brightening ... 'when Glenville goes there'll be no Glenville at all, and at least we have Jim here.'

'Really, Father!" Robin's mother had protested of that 'at least' and on behalf of her uninterested son.

'Young Jim's all right,' Grandfather had conceded, 'the same as his father was.' There had been a moment of silence for the son, husband and father who was not with them any more.

'Also, even if he's not a Robbie,' Grandfather had resumed, 'not a pigheaded Mansfield, he's still a Mansfield in name, and all that the Glenvilles have finished up with is another name.'

'Why?' young Robin had asked, perplexed.

'Because when you marry, young 'un, if you're a girl that follows.'

'I won't, Grandy,' Robin had promised eagerly.

8

'That's my girl. So long, anyway, honey, as it's never Glenville.'

There were no Glenvilles now, but there had been Glenvilles for so long that you still said Glenville. Robin herself had just said the Glenville kid, the boy who must really be old Glenville's step-grandchild, his daughter having died and her husband having remarried in England. The one she had called the boy's father would be the first wife's son. Funny, she thought, that in a small place like Yarani she still did not know his correct surname, but then all Yarani had stuck to Glenville. Even the fine old homestead bore a name that no one bothered about, they always called it Glenville. Everything to do with the property and the family was Glenville.

'What are you called?' she asked the child now.

'Pablo.'

'Pablo?'

'There *is* another name that they say,' the child admitted.

'And from your voice it's George or William or John.'

'Pablo will do.' He looked hopefully at her.

'Right you are, Pablo.' Robin liked children.

'Ragsy for you?'

'We won't be seeing each other again, so Ragsy will do.'

They exchanged knowing grins, and Robin finished her adjusting and rode over to Jim. She saw Pablo . . . who alternatively might be Peter or Paul . . . returning to the jeep on the other side of the boundary fence. The man sat in it now and his finger was on the horn summoning the child. Robin hated people who summoned, she never did it herself, not once at classes had she—

Classes! Good grief, the child might be enrolled there – there was nowhere else for the youngsters in Yarani until they started boarding school. She should have remembered and not agreed to his Pablo, to her Ragsy. But, shrugging, there was little chance of it happening. Even though the Glenvilles, another name now, of course, had not kept the feud red and hot like the Mansfields had, presumably since they viewed it from the favoured end, for it was always easier to be magnanimous when you were on top, they would never ask a Mansfield to teach a Glenville. A Glenville taking lessons from a Mansfield! Robin smiled thinly. The Glenvilles only took land.

She glanced across to the jeep and momentarily met the driver's eyes. Robin enjoyed the sharp, bright vision of many country people who look out a lot, and she focused him distinctly. He stared back as though he saw her equally clearly.

'Decent bloke,' Jim said as Robin rode up. He jerked his head in the direction of the jeep. Pablo had returned, so the horn was not screeching now. At Robin's inflamed glance, Jim sighed and said: 'I had a yarn with him. He's all right. Oh, for Pete's sake, Rob!'

'He's a Glenville,' she protested.

'No, he's a—'

'Still a Glenville. So is the child.'

'The boy is the son of Tamar Warren's stepmother.'

'Is that his name?'

'Yes. Tamar Warren. You knew his name wasn't Glenville.'

'He's a Glenville to me. They all were. Anyway, we never ever saw him when we were brats, did we?'

'No, he was a bit older than us, then mostly away at boarding school when we were home. After that, he got into promotion business, he just told me, and spent years studying overseas. He went right to the top. But his heart was really here.' Jim tried to stop a sigh.

For here, though neither of them ever discussed it, was *not* Robin's twin's heart.

Turning the horses, they started back in the direction of the homestead again.

It was still the same home that Robin had known as a

child. How could it be more, she thought bitterly, when the funds, if not exactly running out, had barely kept pace with the skyrocketing cost of living? Ever since old Glenville had claimed their land and then changed to cattle the Glenvilles had gone ahead, but ever since Grandfather Mansfield had reluctantly turned the land over, keeping to sheep, the Mansfields had stopped still.

Had she been strictly fair, Robin would have admitted that most of the far-westerners had stopped still without any Glenville interference, that many more again had failed altogether and got out. She would have admitted that Glenville's foresight in dropping sheep for cattle at that precise time had put him on the wave of success; admitted, too, that it had not been the forfeit of their land that had been their bad luck but a sudden cessation of the golden days of the fifties, when fleeces had jumped so high in value that Robin remembered Grandfather once showing her a tiny scrap of wool caught in the barbed wire fence and telling her it was worth half a crown.

For it had been half-crowns then, and pounds, shillings and pence, but, like the change in wool, the money had changed. Now it was dollars and cents, just as now it was synthetics. Though—

Though – quickening Ribbons' pace and Jim beside her grumbling mildly as he had to quicken Tudor's – after fifteen years of depression, rising wool prices were putting smiles back on country faces. Only last week the wool industry had bounced back to life in its biggest rise in twenty years. How, thought Robin, would Mr. Cattleman like that?

'He's Warren. Tamar Warren. I told you.' Robin must have spoken Mr. Cattleman aloud, for Jim said it remonstratively.

'Well, how would he like it?' she demanded.

'Very much, I would say.'

'A Glenville like other people prospering!'

'You're Grandfather all over again, and yes, he would. You see, he's keen on more land.'

'A Glenville trait,' Robin interrupted sarcastically.

'And sees,' continued Jim, ignoring her, 'more chance in acquiring it in a boom.' He gave his twin a sidewise look that she did not miss . . . or fail to register. 'We've been talking about that,' he said.

'How could a boom yield him land?' Robin asked quickly; she did not want to linger on what Jim had just quietly implied. 'I should have thought that his time to acquire it would have been during the gloom not the boom.'

'Then you would have been wrong. When wool goes down to twenty-nine cents and a sheep down to fifty, a man knows he can't go down any further, that anyone who will buy will only buy cheap. So' . . . a shrug . . . 'the sheep man hangs on. But when he soars again, it's a different story. The farmer has had an experience that he doesn't want to go through again, and he's ready for *out*.'

'Some,' said Robin.

'Some,' said Jim, and they rode the rest of the way in silence.

Nooroo, meaning speed, though the pace that Grandfather Mansfield had planned for his property had slowed up these latter years, was a homestead in the old style. It was one-level, had a long hall with rooms each side of it, and sat rather hat-like with its wide brim of shady verandah. A few of the more prosperous stations had put up modern places, either pulling down the old homesteads or retaining them for their children's guests when they flew up from Sydney for weekends.

But Nooroo was not prosperous. Nor the Mansfields. At least they had not been since the wool had dropped. They had not been last year. Nor last month. Nor last week. But now – Almost visibly, Robin hugged herself.

No one knew how the miracle had come about, and in their joy they . . . the sheep men . . . were not bothering to

12

question, but practically overnight buying had jumped up again, wool had become king again, or near-king, and what was most important it looked like holding its ground.

We're not rich, Robin knew, not with that bank overdraft to conquer, but the fleece is once more turning to gold.

She turned to her brother as she thought that, opening her mouth to say it, say 'The fleece is turning to gold.' Then she saw his face, and turned back again. Dear Jim, she thought with a pang, surely as unlike to twin brother of mine as any twin brother could be, but lovable, and I love him. – Yet I also love his wife.

What's wrong with Jim and Ginny?

Virginia . . . Ginny . . . was on the verandah waiting for them. Robin saw Jim's quick glance at her, the slight lift to his shoulder, the slight tug to his mouth. He's not happy, Robin knew, and I know Ginny isn't happy either. What went wrong with those two?

She watched her brother cross to her sister-in-law and kiss her, she watched Ginny return the kiss. Window dressing, she thought, something put on for young Robin, for there's nothing *really* there. Nothing magic. Nothing . . . well, nothing as I planned. What is it? It seemed right when it happened. It seemed the answer for both of them. Ginny adrift, Jim purposeless. Oh, why did I bring them together? For, in a way, Robin had.

There had been no room for Robin at Nooroo when schooldays were over. Glancing behind her now to a wide horizon meeting a wide sky, bringing her glance back to a wide house with too many wide rooms, that sounded absurd. What she had really meant by no room had been no position, no occupation – paying occupation. So Robin had stopped in Sydney and clerked.

That was how she had met Ginny. She had answered the ad for a flat-sharer and had fitted Ginny's requirements as to outlook and age.

'Although,' the tall fair girl had laughed, 'we could still fight like cats and dogs. Time will tell. Willing to try it out?'

'I have to find somewhere,' Robin had said.

'Then come. Only' . . . a pause . . . 'it could be that it isn't for long. But at least then you would hold the tenancy of the apartment and could choose your own co-flatter.'

'You might be leaving?'

'Might . . . could . . . it's possible,' Ginny had supplied a little vaguely.

'I'll meet that when it comes,' Robin had offered.

'Good!' Ginny had extended her hand.

They had got on very well. Not in the enthusiastic, embracing way that often ends in disillusion, but quietly, comfortably and companionably.

'We could go on to old-maidship together,' Ginny had said once.

'Perhaps we will.' Because her heart was in Yarani, Robin had not spread herself socially in Sydney. If anything romantic happened, she had always thought, it will have to find me, for I won't be going after it.

'Perhaps, Rob,' Ginny had nodded, 'though—'

Something in her voice had set Robin's eyes directly on her. 'Is this that warning you gave me at our first meeting catching me up?' she asked. 'That hint that you mightn't be staying long?'

'It could be. I'll be telling you definitely anyway tomorrow.'

'A man, of course?'

'Yes. He's been away. Actually he's been away, on and off, mostly off, for years.'

'And you've waited all those long years,' Robin had bantered, for Ginny was only the same age as she was.

'I was quite young when it started,' Ginny had related, 'so in a way you could say years.'

'And now the big moment is looming up?'

14

'It could be.'

'Could be?' Robin had echoed. 'Could be, after all that wasted time? How long-suffering can you get?'

'I haven't suffered. As a matter of fact I—' Ginny had paused, a slight frown on her pretty face. She had looked a little lost.

Robin had pressed her hand but not probed any deeper. 'Time will tell,' she had borrowed from Ginny's greeting on their first day.

The girl had not elaborated, but that was typical of Ginny. Anyone else would have babbled it all out, told the story, given the names. Robin had to piece it together herself.

She had decided that Ginny had met this man on the eve of some course or promotion that he was undertaking, a project that would take him overseas for a period of years. During those years he had evidently returned occasionally, and they had taken up where they had left off. Apparently letters had been exchanged, confidences, schemes, everything exchanged . . . except rings.

They had not been engaged.

Now he was coming home permanently, and Ginny, she supposed, was naturally expecting a permanency for herself. Well, Robin had thought privately, she's welcome to him. Any man who could keep you dangling for five years. . . .

She had watched Ginny getting ready for the dinner to which he was taking her for their reunion, the careful . . . yet somehow nervous . . . attention to her appearance. She's not sure of him, Robin had fumed, after five years she still doesn't know if he'll—

But she had known when Ginny had returned that night. Robin had heard the door click and had listened for two pairs of steps, for she had anticipated that Ginny would bring him up for coffee. There had only been Ginny's.

'Asleep?' Ginny had called.

15

'No. Come in.'

Ginny had come. She had sat on Robin's bed. 'No need to advertise for a new flatter,' she had announced simply.

'That's nice.' Robin had used simplicity in return. 'I prefer you.' But her eyes had raked Ginny's face. She looked tired, she had thought, she looked at the end of something. Men, Robin had seethed, all men all over the world, except old Grandfather who was dead now, and, of course, Jim.

Jim!

Jim was coming down next week to see his agent. Ginny should appeal to Jim, he was the same reticent type.

Because Ginny was characteristically offering no details, Robin had asked for none. But she had said eagerly: 'Seeing you're not leaving, I was wondering—'

'Yes?'

'My brother has to come down from Yarani. It would be wonderful if we could let him bunk on the divan. The plain sad fact, Ginny, is this: He isn't rolling.'

'Who wants money?' Ginny had said, and Robin had put another piece to her story: evidently 'that man' had still wanted to chase the dollar, or the know-how to collect the dollar, and Ginny, once more, had been set aside.

'Then Jim can come?'

'Of course.'

'You'll like Jim,' she had said, 'he'll like you.'

It had been a remarkable understatement, Robin had found to her joy when later the thing had happened (though now, uneasily, she was less joyful) for it had proved much more than liking.

Ginny and her brother had been married within a week.

The front door was wide open so that any breeze that

could be coaxed from the still hot day would find its way down the long hall. Ginny led them to the big kitchen, where the first Mansfields had eaten, and, since there had been little money since then to put into the house for it had been needed first to maintain the station, the present Mansfields also ate.

Robin had never bothered about it, but she knew Ginny did not like it. She knew that everything on the Mansfield station had been rather a shock to Ginny. She was a very fastidious girl. Her taste was excellent. Even the small Sydney flat, though decorated on a meagre budget, had been a delight. There, Robin remembered, throwing her things on the big old table around which they used to eat, and still ate, though only at one corner now, Ginny had had a separate dining alcove fixed up. She had said she didn't like looking at saucepans when she took her meals. Now she had to. But, and thank heaven at least for this, the girl was not back on the early bête noir days, the times of the big black fuel stoves. She would have loathed that.

She was a wonderful cook, if strictly of the gourmet class. Because the station had reduced its stock, the shearers this year had come in a small parcel, and without a cook. Ginny had been called upon to fill the role. Robin sighed as she remembered the top man coming to her one day and complaining about the corned mutton. He said the corned dog.

'We've had it every day, miss.'

'Jim will be killing again on Friday.' Her brother, Robin had thought, should have seen to it before, but he hated killing and tended to put it off.

'It's not that we're complaining about, not fresh meat — it's the dog, always the same, cold with beetroot or tomatoes.'

'Oh! All right, I'll tell Mrs. Mansfield,' Robin had reassured the man.

It had not been hard telling her, Ginny was not a

touchy person, just a quietly unhappy one.

'Oh, dear,' her sister-in-law, Ginny who could turn out cordon bleu dishes, had admitted, 'but what other way is there?'

'Ways, pet. Curried dog, shepherd's pie dog, dog croquettes, dog patties.'

'Oh, I am sorry.' Ginny had got to work at once and made a fine job, the men had applauded her, come for seconds, in all it had been a welcome diversion. But then the shearing had been over and the routine had settled back again. With luck, and the way the winds of fortune seemed to be blowing now, that would be their last small shearing. The next parcel of shearers would be a large one, and have to bring their own cook. Because, Robin, thought, after we discharge our debts we'll build up our stock again. The fleece is once more turning gold.

Jim had poured cold beers and they sat at the table drinking them. Ginny, Robin guessed, would have preferred sherry in a delicately stemmed glass . . . and I believe Jim would, too. But Yarani isn't that kind of place.

Staring through the window at golden-green grass that seemed to turn blue as it neared the lilac horizon, Robin wondered a little uneasily whether it was herself to blame and not Yarani. If she had not been here, would Ginny have taken out her delicate glasses that she never had unpacked? It could be me, Robin knew, dressed as I am in khaki shirt, khaki trews, no compliment for a dainty hostess. But after all, they both begged me to come. Odd, that, she thought for the first time, a young couple needing a third.

For Jim had said: 'I could do with you, Rob, you're as good as a man – better, really, for you get yourself involved.'

'I am involved,' Robin had pointed out. 'I'm always involved when it's Yarani. But money, Jim?' Three meals a day is all I'd ask just to be up here, but I know my independent brother.'

'You're right, I'd have to pay you something, otherwise it would be no go. But it could only be so little. However,' Jim went on, 'I've been listening around the district. Do you know there are nine teachable kids, but all too young yet for boarding school?'

'I can't teach,' Robin pointed out.

'You can superintend their correspondence lessons, and there's not a parent who wouldn't throw in for that. You know how our own mother found it a bore. Say two or three days a week.'

'You're tempting me,' smiled Robin.

'I want to. How otherwise can I take my city Ginny up there? Up to the wilderness? Mother's leaving, you know.'

Yes, Robin did know. As soon as Mrs. Mansfield had heard the news of her son she had said happily: 'At last I can get out!' She had said goodbye to Ginny and Jim thankfully, kissed Robin joyfully, and had left for the Melbourne suburb where she had lived before she had married, and where her sister still lived, almost at once. Poor dear Mum! Oh, goodness, Robin thought, I'm showering 'poors' on everyone today. Actually it should be poor Robin, for something ominous is coming, I feel it in the air. It won't be long now before Jim says—

'Please come, Rob,' her brother had entreated after the ceremony, and when Ginny had backed him up, Robin had.

She recalled Ginny looking round her that first day, looking at the golden emptiness, but not seeing it as Robin did, because, Robin supposed, you had to be born into it to look at it like that. Yet Jim had been born into it, too, but he—

She mused on the differences in a family. Grandfather Mansfield, fiercely land, his son, Jim senior, the father Robin could barely remember, only mildly so, then Jim milder still. But Robin a born 'Me, too', as Jim had said, a second Grandfather M.

She wondered if all families had these changes within them. For some reason she wondered about the Glenvilles. Old Glenville would have been the land type, but she did not know about his daughter. According to Jim, the grandson, Tamar Warren, had inherited the urge. Jim had said: 'Here was his heart.' And later: 'He's keen on more land.'

And that, sensed Robin, was to be the trend when Jim spoke again. *Really* spoke, not just touched around things as he had before.

Ginny was setting the table, taking dainty dishes from the stove. She was chattering about things she had heard on the wireless today, but every now and then she darted Jim a prompting look. Presently she announced dinner and they sat round.

The conversation was bright enough, but it was not the conversation that Robin remembered, and had loved. Always Grandfather had set the pattern: the clip, the fences, the rain or the absence of rain. Never city snippets as heard on the radio.

It all comes down to this, that I should have been born the boy, Robin thought; this is my life, here I belong. Jim, bless him, has never belonged.

For a few moments she thought sympathetically about Jim. Naturally the station had gone to him ... who else? ... so just as naturally as soon as his elementary schooling had been over, he had attended agricultural college. *I* would have loved it, Robin knew, but Jim was the man of the house, so he had to go, and he always hated it.

She looked at Jim lovingly. Only a kind person like he was would have worn that worried expression – worried, she knew, for her. It was his place entirely, he had absolutely no need to confer with her, he was the Mansfield male, and that was all that mattered. Grandfather, she remembered, had explained it all to her once when she was young. It had been during the fifties boom, and

Grandfather had said: 'The man of the house, of course, always inherits. In which case, young Robbie, I'm trying to make up to you by choosing you the very top school.'

'I don't want it,' Robin had said. 'I only want Yarani.'

'Perhaps when you've done,' Grandfather, had continued carefully avoiding the subject of Yarani, adding more sugar to the pill, 'a world trip.'

There had been no world trip, the money had gone down by then, but Robin had been aware that her school had been much more expensive than Jim's. Probably Ginny's, too. Yet look at the expensive ex-schoolgirl now, sitting at the table in khaki shirt and trews, work-soiled and stained at that.

She glanced back to Jim, and at once, twin-like, she read his wish to re-open the subject that he had skirted around on their ride home, but was too considerate to continue now. Dear unselfish Jim, she thought, and because any Nooroo change, though she knew it must eventually come, was so vague, so distant, so indistinct somehow, she encouraged confidently:

'You're over-considering me, aren't you, brother? It's entirely your place, remember.'

Jim looked at her gratefully, grateful that at least she had broken the ice, had brought the subject up. 'I fetched you back here, Rob,' he reminded her.

'Then you can jolly well take me back again to the city when you go,' Robin said flippantly; she was still unconcerned, everything was still a long, comfortable way off.

But his answer was not flippant, and any lightness Robin had tried to imbue into the subject broke down as her twin said:

'And it could be soon, young Rob. Tamar Warren and I have agreed to negotiate a price.'

CHAPTER TWO

Somehow, and very stupidly, Robin now knew, not at any time, even after Jim had mentioned it, had she seriously considered a Glenville as a buyer. She should have kept in mind that their properties touched, that any landowner wishing to acquire more land would naturally prefer to extend, but always when she had thought about it, and that had been rarely, it had been Sam Williams on the further side of Glenville's who had come to her mind for Glenville acquisition, never their own Nooroo. She recalled, too, that Sam Williams, elderly now, children married and left, had wanted to get away.

She must have mumbled this aloud, for Jim said: 'Warren has already acquired the Williams land.'

'Then he's a shark,' she scowled.

'His cattle is mostly Brahma, and those fellows take up a hell of a lot of space.'

'Perhaps they do, but you wouldn't even think of it, Jim,' Robin said confidently, still not believing that damning 'Tamar Warren and I have agreed to negotiate a price'; forgetting how magnanimous she had been to her twin just now in the belief that she could well afford to, that it was all in the very distant future.

'Robin, I've *thought*.' Jim brought her up with a jerk. 'I've just told you – we've reached the final stage.'

'Reached it with a Glenville!'

'He's Tamar Warren.'

'But still a Glenville,' Robin insisted.

'What of it?'

'Grandfather would turn in his grave.'

'Grandfather,' said Jim. Then he said no more.

They left it at that. It needed airing, discussing, arguing, but they were both too touchy and on edge to begin.

Robin got up, called, 'I'm tired,' avoided Jim's anxious face, Ginny's wistful look, and went to her room.

She undressed, slipped into a gown, put out the light, then went and sat at the window, sat as she had sat as a child, loving it now as she had loved it then. The navy blue evening lit only by star sprinkles and a wedge of moon encompassed her, enfolded her to it much more than the glittering lights reflected in the harbour that had been Ginny's pretty offering had ever done. She loved the dark, the strange movements in the dark, the cry of a nightjar, pheasants calling to each other, wood pigeons cooing. Then a marauding wallaby might rustle the branches of a tree, one of the dogs stir in his sleep. I guess you could say, thought Robin, I'm simply and basically a country girl, 'corn-fed', Grandfather used to tease, only we don't grow it. Now I wonder if we did ... I've thought, too, about a sunflower crop; the seeds are selling well.

She stopped herself sternly. No plans, she thought, it never was yours, it isn't, and it won't be. Nooroo is not even going to be 'related' to you, it's going to be sold to a stranger, and of all strangers— To be sold was bad enough, to a stranger was worse, but to a Glenville it was – Why, it was damnable! Robin seethed.

Jim had sounded very decisive tonight – the first time, really, that she remembered her twin taking a stand. If she could keep that obduracy in mind, she could fight him back ... not that she could legally, of course, for the place was entirely his. But she could be the little stinker that at heart she rather suspected – no, *knew* she was when it came to Nooroo. But it would be hard when your opponent was Jim, Jim who, for all his determination, was still sensitive enough *not* to make a move without her support.

She pleated the voile curtain hanging soft and straight in the windless air. Why did Jim want to sell right now, now when their tide of fortune could be turning? All she could conclude was that Glenville's ... *Warren's* ... price was very good. Oh, she knew Jim disliked the land, and Ginny's dislike must be a final straw, but now, now when the wool clip was right down, making any available wool like gold, down because of the massive slaughter of sheep through lack of demand, through drought, through the invasion of synthetics, through the inevitable drift away of the land man from sheep that had reduced the sheep population by twenty millions, now was the time to hold, not sell. Yet Jim maintained that now was the time for a good price. He had said it with a desperation as well as a hardness. And Robin knew the desperation would touch her where the hardness never would. She knew in the end she would agree. But to a Glenville! she grimaced. She turned away from the window to her bed.

She did not sleep with her usual ease. Having tossed and drifted between thoughts and dreams all night, she awoke unrefreshed. It was a schoolday, too, but out here it did not matter very much since scholastic results were not expected; the mothers were simply grateful to have the children taken off their hands so they could assist where assistance was needed, outside paid help being considerably reduced during the latter leaner years.

Just as well dresses, stockings and fashionable shoes were not called for, Robin thought, getting into the clean but frayed jodhpurs and shirt she always wore since she never knew what she would be called upon to do, for her stock of female attire had gone down. But this gear was far more suitable. Once during a fierce little willy-willy the small outside toilet had floated upward and had had to be reached down and then moored with all the ropes and weights she could find. Once five-year-old Trevor had decided he had had enough school for the day and she had had to gallop a mile after him and return him in front of her on Ribbons. Once she had had to remove a dead frog from the school tank. Twice she had had snakes to deal with. So she had given away feminine stuff.

Today she drove the jeep; she had some equipment to

take to the schoolhouse that Ginny had done for her. Ginny loved doing it. She liked sitting at the table and cutting out things and pasting them in. She was an inside girl, Robin thought fondly. Poor Ginny!

She arrived at the tiny building at the same time as three child-delivering cars. They brought two scholars apiece. The other three pupils were older, and rode their ponies.

There was no explicit starting time. Robin stood around talking with the mothers until the mothers, feeling guilty about the things they could be doing, drove home again. As Robin watched them go she knew, and felt glad for them, that their tide was turning. The dark days were over, soon they would be advertising for companion-governesses once more, enjoying the diversion of another woman around the house, leaving her in charge when they went down to Sydney on a shopping spree.

Robin went into the schoolroom. It was small but cheerful. Ginny, bless her, had made a set of murals, had run up some bright curtains. The chairs and tables were surplus furniture that the different homesteads had donated, and Ginny had painted then ornamented them with pasted nursery animals. In all it was a happy domain.

There was no set routine. How could there be with only two pupils of the nine at the same standard? Robin put the older ones to their correspondence lessons, the tinies to the sand-tray and building blocks, and the in-betweens, the ones she found hardest since they were out of finger painting and teddy bear hugging yet not quite into reading, to elementary numbers.

She liked the work. Had she not left her heart at Yarani, she believed she would have chosen teaching. As it had turned out, she had agreed to be a clerk. Much quicker for only a short time, she had thought, feeling that any job was only a stand-in until she came back.

Well, she had come back, but now, or so it appeared,

she was going away again. Away from Yarani. Dear, dear Yarani.

'Robin' . . . in an intimate school like this there was no 'Miss Mansfield' . . . 'you dropped water into my paint. It was a nice bright blue and now it's yukky.' The voice was young and complaining.

'I'm sorry, Dilys.'

'Why did you cry into my nice blue?'

'I didn't, Dilys.'

'Well, something ran over from your eye.'

'Something's running over the hill,' announced Tim. They called it the hill, actually saw a hill in it, but unless you came from Yarani and from familiarity could detect that inch, barely more, rise in the terrain you would have said there was no difference.

Robin glanced through the window and saw it was a car. It must be coming out here, for the track ended here. She unlocked the desk and saw that the little pistol she had been trained in handling was conveniently placed. She had refused it at first when the fathers, because of the schoolhouse's isolation, had requested it, she had pointed out tactfully that not one of the children just now could have fetched a ransom had it been a kidnapper who called, but all the same she had seen their wisdom, then finally agreed. As she placed the small weapon to her satisfaction and locked the drawer carefully again, she thought of the new circumstances that could now arise; there could be plenty of money for ransom if wool soared up again. However – shrugging – she and the little isolated schoolhouse would not be needed then, there would be governesses for hire.

'It's Mr. Warren,' said one of the girls.

Young Jack said: 'And that pommie kid.'

'English, John,' Robin corrected.

'He talks with a prune in his mouth.'

'He speaks beautifully.' – I only hope, Robin added to herself, he doesn't call me Ragsy. She wondered why she was being visited.

She went to the door, then out to the yard, away from the curious ears of children. The car was just pulling up. Pablo got out first ... no, *not* Pablo, she disciplined herself.

The man followed.

It was odd to think that never in her life had she really seen her neighbour before (except yesterday at the boundary fence) when he belonged as near as next door, had done so for many years. Yet next door was miles away, and, being older, the man, as a boy, would have been away at boarding school, then, when she and Jim reached that stage themselves, away carving himself a career. Promotion or something, Jim had said it was. Apart from travelling in a city or Yarani-bound train with him, and no doubt a Glenville always drove or flew, there would have been little likelihood of meeting him, or knowing if they did. Also, he appeared a kind of person not to participate in Yarani's few local gatherings; he appeared another arrogant Glenville, for to Robin all Glenvilles had to be arrogant.

She tried to remember old Glenville, but it was too far back. She had a hazy impression of an angry red face and bristling moustaches, but this man's face was brown and had no moustache, and though you would not call the countenance exactly amiable, on the other hand there was no anger – not, anyway, just now. For the rest, he was tall, broad-shouldered and carried himself like a man, Robin thought ungraciously, who put his finger on car norns to summon children. Arrogant, she judged again.

'Good morning,' she said.

'Good morning.'

'Did you want something?' from Robin.

'Yes. To speak to Miss Mansfield.'

'I'm Miss Mansfield.'

'I'm Tamar Warren,' the man said.

If he had come about Nooroo—

'I've come to enrol Mathew' ... so Pablo was Mathew ... 'if you'll accept him. Mathew, say good morning to Miss Mansfield.'

The tow-haired little boy looked innocently up at Robin and intoned, 'Good morning, Miss Mansfield.'

'Good morning, Mathew.' Robin turned to Tamar Warren.

'I'm not a qualified teacher.'

'No.' His glance was travelling up and down her working shirt and jodphurs. To her own annoyance Robin heard herself defending:

'I wear these because—'

'That's all right,' he said patronizingly.

There was a moment's silence, broken by Pablo.

'Can I go and meet the class?'

Tamar Warren looked at Robin.

'He's your child,' she indicated.

'Stepbrother,' he corrected. 'But it's your school. You can go only if Miss Mansfield says so, Mathew.'

'Yes, Mathew,' Robin said.

When Robin had galloped over, she repeated to the man, 'I don't teach, I just supervise the correspondence lessons.'

'Mathew hasn't any. It could be that he won't be in this country long enough to bother. However, I don't object to him borrowing some of the existent ones if you, and the owner of them, also don't object.'

'That is if I accept him,' Robin edged in.

'Any reason not to?'

'If he's not to be here long—'

'But then' ... smoothly ... 'perhaps *you* won't be, Miss Mansfield.'

It was the first edge forward to the subject of Nooroo, and Robin stepped back. Stepped back actually as well as in her mind. Doing so, she slipped. One of the children had left out a toy. But for the man's hand, she would have fallen over. He held it a little longer to make sure she had regained her balance. Annoyed at the flush she could feel flaming her cheeks, Robin pulled away, the jerkiness of the gesture only deepening the flush and making it more apparent still. She heard his low, amused little laugh.

'Dangerous,' he said aloud of the toy. 'However, I do appreciate how hard it must be to look after everything, to supervise a number of children all of different ages. Despite all this, could you take on another?'

'For a short time only,' she said stiffly.

'I told you that was probable, anyway. Mathew will be rejoining his mother . . . his *parents* then.'

'Anyway, as you pointed out, possibly I won't be here,' Robin slipped in slyly.

'No, I expect with the wool boom again, a governess in the home once more will be the regular and accepted thing.'

'I said *I* won't be here.' She looked directly at him, and then all around her. Looked significantly.

He raised his brows in maddening inquiry.

'You should know,' she said tersely. 'You're negotiating with my brother.'

'Oh, so he's told you?'

'He generally does.'

He did not comment on that. He regarded her thoughtfully a moment, several moments, in fact it was Robin, finally, who looked away.

'Will you accept Mathew?' were his words when at last he spoke to her. 'He's companion-hungry. I haven't met my stepmother yet, but if she's as outgoing as this boy—'

'I'll accept him,' Robin said formally. She was relieved, yet at the same time disappointed, that he had not followed up the other. 'The fee is—' She told him.

'Very reasonable. How do you put up with them for so little?'

'Multiplied by nine . . . ten now . . . it becomes more. I find it sufficient, anyhow.'

'I would still require a larger amount.'

'It's enough. Did you want to see the classroom? The schooldays are Monday, Wednesday, Friday. Nine to four. Tell Pab— have your housekeeper pack a lunch. If you have any spare white paper could Mathew bring it? The smaller ones get through all the drawing material I can find. Would you care to pay now?'

'Yes.' He put his hand in his pocket. 'I must say, Miss Mansfield,' he remarked, 'you're easier to deal with than your brother. You do get things done.'

'I feel they get done to me. Shall I call Mathew out?'

'I hoped you would start him today. Would that be an extra fee?' Again his hand went to his pocket.

'Yes, you can leave him, but no, it's no extra. Please don't be late calling for him this afternoon, as it holds me up, and I have a lot to do at Nooroo now that—' Annoyed again at herself, she broke off.

'I'll call on the dot.' The man turned back to the car and took out a lunch packet. 'I brought it in case,' he grinned.

But Robin did not smile. She accepted the packet, nodded to the man, then turned back to the schoolhouse. She knew that he was watching her, that he watched her right to the door. She was inside the room before the car took off.

She found Mathew perfectly at home already. He was describing to the class how he didn't mind pommie as it meant cheeks like apples.

'Well, yours aren't,' pointed out one of the children. 'You have freckles.' He had, too, noted Robin; his fair English skin had attracted them at once.

'Brown tan is only freckles all joined together,' said Mathew knowledgeably. 'Indian braves started off with freckles that grew.'

The class liked him; he was, as his stepbrother had said, very outgoing.

'I'll show you the washbasin,' Robin offered, and once

she got him to the verandah began to tell him never, *never* to call her Ragsy, not here. But he was too quick for her to finish the instruction.

'I've decided I'll be that other name,' he said, 'that Mathew, and keep Pablo and Ragsy for just us.'

'Yes, I'm Robin, you're Mathew.'

'Robin,' he agreed, 'but after flowers, not birds.' He went happily back to class.

The day went on as their schooldays always did. Singsong. Games. Lunch together. A short nature walk. Rest period.

Then the small riders were saddling up for home, the other mothers coming in their cars to collect their children.

As before, Robin stood talking to them. The Gillespies were going to avail themselves of the higher selling prices and get out. 'A shop round the corner, a dentist when you want him,' Peggy Gillespie gloated. One mother agreed. One mother said they would stop for the good times when they came. One by one the three departed and Robin was left with Mathew. She was annoyed at being kept, there was much to do at Nooroo, for Ginny had never got into the habit of seeing to the few hens they kept, and Wattie, their aged rouseabout, had his hands filled with the several cows and pigs. Jim would be out in the paddocks again, they had had trouble with several fences. Yet this man chose to upset her working plans.

But she was careful not to let Pablo see her annoyance. She had a suspicion that underneath all that outgoing, there was an extremely sensitive little boy.

'He's late,' Mathew said at last.

'Something must be keeping him.' To herself Robin added angrily that his lateness also would not bother Mr. Cattleman.

'I think he doesn't want me much,' said Mathew.

'He's your brother.'

'Only a step. It's not like this step.' Mathew was standing on one as he waited. 'It's different. It's when your mother gets married.' He stopped abruptly at that, and Robin had the feeling that if she turned and looked at him she would see a tear.

'Yes,' she said as casually as she could, but she did *not* feel casual about Tamar Warren. What kind of unfeeling brute must he be to make the child wait like this? Admittedly the boy was no blood relation, but—

'I tell you what, darling,' Robin proposed, 'I'll drive you, it's on my way. I'm next door, remember?'

She was next door, but the Glenvilles were not on her way; she always took the back track as it was shorter. However, Mathew seemed cheered up, and ran across and climbed into the jeep.

They took off in golden dust across golden countryside, mostly cleared paddocks, but always a tree to trace patterns on the ground, eucalypt trees, red, silver, umbrella, scribbly.

'Do you like it?' Robin asked the little boy, wondering how his young English eyes saw this golden, not green, scene.

'Yes. But—'

He was homesick. Either that or mother-sick. Clearly Robin saw it. Yet that pig . . .

She dug her foot down on the accelerator and succeeded in letting off some of her steam as well as divert Mathew. He clapped his hands at the racing paddocks, the flashing bushes. They came to the gate of the Glenville homestead almost within minutes.

Robin hesitated then. The last thing she wanted to do was go in, yet it must be half a mile to the house, a long walk for a little boy who had used up a lot of energy today, too much energy really, and Robin frowned over that. The child was almost over-active, probably, if unwittingly, seeking escape from the painful knowledge that he was far away from home.

She glanced up the drive – no gummy peppercorns as

at Nooroo, but elegant pines. A Glenville *would* plant pines and not peppercorns, Robin thought. You could still see the house in spite of the long drive, though, because the building was so large. Unlike most country houses, it was two storeys. No long hall with rooms each side for the affluent Glenvilles.

Pablo was scrambling out to open the gate, at least his brother had taught him that, but then wouldn't it be the first thing, the driver sitting regally back, that a Glenville ... *Warren* ... would teach? Robin resigned herself distastefully to entering the enemy's territory, then she exclaimed happily: 'No, Mathew, no need, here's Mr. Warren now.' The Warren car was coming down between the pines.

Robin reversed her own car ready to return home, and would have done so without encountering Tamar Warren had not a finger gone down on the horn again. Angered, she felt like disobeying the summons ... what a man he was for summoning! ... but the child was there, and he restricted her. About to release the brake, she stopped. But she did not reverse back to the gate again. Let him walk across, she thought.

He did so ... after he had put his little stepbrother into his own car. As he approached her, she saw that his shoulders were hunched now, that he looked unmistakably drawn.

'Is there anything wrong, Mr Warren?' she asked in spite of herself as he came up.

'Yes.'

'Can I help?'

'I think ... and I hope ... you can.'

'Then tell me.'

'It could take a bit longer than the boy's patience would allow.' He glanced back to his own car. 'I'm sorry you were kept back this afternoon. Can I come across and see you tonight?'

'See me?'

'Yes.'

'Come across where?'

'To your homestead.'

'To Nooroo?' she queried.

'Yes.'

'But—' Robin began.

'I can't have you here, I don't want him to know – not just yet.'

'It all sounds mysterious.'

He said a little hopelessly, 'No, nothing like that. Anyway, I have to see your brother regardless. I thought that ordinarily – and very probably – as soon as *I* turned up, you would get up and walk out.'

'Ordinarily and very probably yes,' she said coldly. That admission that he had to see Jim had chilled her, for she knew *why*. Nooroo, of course.

'So will you please not, Miss Mansfield,' Tamar Warren was saying. 'There's something I want to ask you afterwards.'

'Ask me afterwards?'

'Yes. Since it all depends, of course, on the outcome of your brother's and my discussion.'

'You mean whether Jim sells or not,' she said bluntly.

'Exactly,' he answered directly. 'Because whatever evolves, a sale or not, I don't want *you* to leave just yet. I didn't turn up today because I was occupied with something else, with the receiving and sending of cables. Miss Mansfield' ... the first definite break-down she had seen in this arrogant man ... 'I've had word from England that my father is dying. I'm not asking you to share that, but I am asking your help with—' He nodded to the car.

'Of course,' she said readily, 'but—'

'Then I can see you afterwards tonight?'

'Yes,' Robin agreed. What else could she do?

As he turned back, she turned the jeep and left.

She was not expected home the way that she came today. It was also a different time from her usual hour. Even before she heard the voices, Ginny's and Jim's voices, Robin sensed the unconcealed despair in the house, unconcealed since they did not know she was there, so had no need to hide anything.

'It's just no use, Jim,' Ginny was crying.

'I know. *I know*. But, Ginny, how can I—'

'How can she, you mean. How can Robin still want this life? It's so lonely, so empty, so impossible, so—'

'She marches to a different drummer,' Jim reminded her.

The different drummer. The drummer to whose beat Grandfather Mansfield had marched, and now Robin. Robin knew in that moment that Jim who did not hear the beat that she heard should not, must not, be penalized for that. She knew that it would all have to finish that way, anyhow, in the end. Probably some small disaster, some minor domestic tragedy had sparked up the present fire. Maybe Ginny, because Robin had not arrived in time, had taken over the feeding of the fowls and left the gate open. One of those small things that build up to a last thing could have happened, because the tension was quite electric now, the atmosphere near-catastrophic. They can't stay here much longer, Robin faced up, not like this, their nerves taut, ready to snap.

She had always been aware that Jim had hated it all. Whereas school vacations had been something precious to look forward to for her, Jim had dreaded them. As for Ginny, she was not, and never would be, a country-woman. Robin had hoped that Ginny's feelings for Jim would help her through, but when Jim had no feeling for Nooroo himself, then how could you keep on hoping like that? Especially when you did not know, as at first Robin had believed she had known, how they really felt for each other. I don't know at all, Robin thought, and it was a bleak thought, all I know is I must give in, I must get them away.

She escaped unseen to her room, then sat down on her bed. It had to come, she knew. Even when I was planning more stock, putting in corn and planting sunflowers I really knew that. Nooroo is not mine. Only the love for it is. But Jim must come before that love, Jim and Ginny. I have to tell them, and tell what I do tell very convincingly, otherwise they'll remain that considerate pair, considerate to me.

What to say?

The school? Complain that she was fed up with it? Grumble that the pupils had been little fiends? No, they both knew her attachment to children.

Perhaps suddenly she could be wishful for the city, for all the attractions that the bright lights offered. No, Ginny knew her too well for that.

A straight-out announcement that she was going to leave? But they were astute, that pair, they could suspect she had overheard them, and be obdurate.

A desire for money? . . . but then she was not entitled to any of Jim's return from the sale.

It had to be something very convincing. She heard the voices still in the kitchen, but did not listen now. She knew the trend. Also, all at once she had decided what it would be. It was preposterous, but it could work . . .

She rose, went to the door, went out to her brother and his wife. For she knew at last what she was going to say.

She sat on the table edge and grinned at them. 'If you want a note for my being late I'll have – Tamar Warren write me one.'

'Tamar Warren?' It was Ginny, and a little sharply.

'The Glenville station, Ginny – I've always spoken of him as Glenville before, we all do.' Jim was looking across at his twin. 'What would the note say?' he asked carefully.

'That you two might be leaving Yarani soon but that I won't.' Robin looked at Jim and waited.

'I won't leave without you, Robin.'

'Nothing in the will says that.'

'You know what I mean.'

'I know what you mean, darling, and I thank you, but I'm still staying here while you two leave.' She heard herself say it, and wondered, a little hysterically, what she would hear herself say next.

Then she heard: 'You see, I've had an offer.' Well, it could be called one in a way. Tamar Warren had said he needed her help, and for help you had to offer something in return.

'And you're going to take it?' It was Ginny again, a little sharply as before.

'Well – yes.'

'You – you mean you don't mind what I intend to do, Robbie? Sell Nooroo?' It was Jim now.

'Oh, I mind.' She was careful not to be too extravagant. Jim would never accept that. 'But not so much, Jim. You see, I won't be going . . . well, not going with you two, anyhow.' She would probably go on the next train, she thought, but with luck they would believe her now, and now was all that mattered.

'Will you tell us?' they begged.

'Not just this moment. Tamar' . . . she deliberately lingered over the name . . . 'is coming round tonight.'

'Yes. It's to—' began her twin.

'I know all about it. And' . . . a gulp Robin hoped Jim didn't notice . . . 'you have my blessing.'

'I just can't believe it,' Jim said after a few stunned minutes. He added bemusedly, 'Of course you must come and live with us, Rob. That is, if you—'

'If ever I leave here,' she finished smoothly for him, and incredulous, but at the same time incredibly relieved, they accepted that.

Ginny began fixing the evening meal . . . but for someone, thought Robin, who had just got her wish, she seemed a little uncertain somehow, confused. Robin wondered about it, but her twin was certainly not wondering about anything. He had become an entirely different man. He looked across the table at his sister and grinned, grinned like he used to a million years ago, Robin thought.

The meal was eaten. The clock hand went round. Tamar Warren's car pulled up and Tamar Warren came in. He was duly introduced to Ginny. Ginny and Robin went out on the verandah while the men talked.

When they came out at last, Ginny excused herself and went in to make supper. Jim went eagerly after her.

Then Robin looked across at Tamar Warren.

A silence encompassed them, it lasted quite a while. When it was finally broken, they both broke it at once.

'It's this way—' Warren said.

'Did Jim agree?' Robin asked.

They both stopped.

It was Tamar who spoke first the next time.

'Jim agreed unconditionally. I was a little surprised, actually, even though I knew he would in the end. I'd expected some discussion.'

'I'd told him to say yes,' Robin explained.

'He said so,' nodded Warren. He paused. 'He also mentioned that he wouldn't have conceded so promptly had you not informed him that you'd had an offer to remain here, an offer that you intended to take.'

'Yes.'

'I was a little dashed,' Warren continued, 'you see, Miss Mansfield, what I had intended to ask you tonight—'

'Offer, please, not ask,' Robin corrected, 'for that's the word I used on Jim and Ginny. I had to do something to move Jim. I hated doing it, but I had to. So . . . well, I said what I did.'

'Concerning an offer?'

'Yes.'

'From whom?'

She looked down, then up once more. 'You.' She

38

waited for an outburst. But none came.

'Then you did right,' he said coolly. 'There is an offer. An offer to become engaged to me, Miss Mansfield.' He waited. Then: 'Would that offer fit the bill, do you think?'

CHAPTER THREE

'I BELIEVE it's generally marriage that's offered, not engagement,' Robin said after a long silence. She could not believe she had heard aright, yet Tamar Warren was still waiting for an answer, so she must have heard *something*. 'Engagement,' she added a little foolishly, 'is the state that comes with the offer.' As earlier in the evening with Ginny and Jim, she seemed to be listening to herself speak, not knowing what she would hear next.

'If you're trying to tell me that that's a stipulation to your agreement,' he said calmly, 'I'll agree in my turn. I'll alter the terms.' At her bewildered look he prompted: 'You don't appear to be following me. I'll accept that inclusion of marriage.'

'You must be crazy!' she gasped.

'It was you who raised the point.'

'And you who agreed to it. All I can say, Mr. Warren, is that you must be a very desperate man.'

'That, Miss Mansfield, is less than complimentary to yourself.'

'I would never marry you.'

'Yet you would become engaged to me?'

'No.'

'But you just said you would accept my offer.'

'I didn't know it was that,' she protested.

'Yet I think you had a kind of idea,' he suggested slyly. 'Your brother seemed to think the same.'

'Jim couldn't. He would be very conscious of how little I knew you.'

'But didn't he do rather the same thing himself?' Warren asked.

She looked at him incredulously. 'Jim told you that?' It was not in character with her reticent twin. In her sur-

40

prise she did not notice that for his reply Tamar Warren made a change of point.

'Perhaps I should have given the offer its right name, Miss Mansfield,' he said, 'an *assumed* engagement for an *assumed* marriage. How do you read that?'

'I don't, until I know more.'

'Fair enough,' he agreed amiably.

A silence took over again. Robin broke it.

'You're not serious?' she disbelieved.

'Very serious. I just added assumed, Miss Mansfield. Remember?'

'Even then you can't be serious.'

'I am. I'm asking you to be a partner in an engagement that will lead to nowhere but benefit several parties in its purposeless journey.'

'Can't you be more explicit?' she asked.

'I can if you'll give me a hearing. No, not here, we're too public.'

'But Ginny and Jim—'

'Will think what we want them to think,' he said calmly.

'You mean—'

'I mean engaged couples don't hang around on exposed verandahs on starry nights waiting to be served supper.' He had the tips of his fingers under her elbow by now and the feel was cool and detached. The lack of warmth, the lack of interest, gave Robin the initiative to leave the house with him and not hang back like an uncertain and gauche child. Which, she thought wryly, she actually was; she was completely inexperienced in this love . . . no, this mock love . . . business.

They walked under the trees to an old wooden bench, but not so romantically dark as it sounded, for a bright slat of light from the house illumined it.

Once there, Tamar Warren did not waste time.

'You don't wish to leave Yarani for the city until you have to,' he said, crisply, 'at the same time I don't want you to go until I'm ready for it. It's all as simple as that.'

'*My* wish is simple,' Robin contributed, 'it's understandable, but you—'

'I want to stay,' he stated, 'so that Mathew can stay. It's very important to me.'

'I didn't think you were so attached to him,' she said sarcastically.

'Let me finish, please. It's very important to me, since my father is incurably ill.'

'Yes, you said so. But—'

'I've never met my stepmother, Mathew's mother, but she sounds a rather special person, and I know that only someone very special would attract my father.'

Robin said quietly, 'You're very attached to your father, aren't you?'

'Does that surprise you?'

'Of course not.' A pause. 'I can barely remember mine.'

'So I've heard.'

'Heard talk,' she murmured mechanically. She said: 'Then the Glenvilles used to gossip about the Mansfields like we gossiped about them?'

'Yes. But kindlier, I think.'

'But then it's easy to be kindlier when you're on the winning side.'

'Yes,' he agreed blandly, and she positively squirmed in her resentment of him.

'Why is it so important that Pab— that Mathew stays here?' she asked presently.

'Because the nature of my father's illness requires my stepmother's entire attention, which naturally she couldn't give if the boy was with her.'

'Then you could keep him with you, you could put him into a school.'

'She would never agree to that. He's her son, her only chick. She's torn by having him away from her as it is, but if she knows he's happy, or as near happy as he can be—'

'You think I can make him that?'

'Yes.'

'But we've barely met.'

'I still think it,' Tamar Warren said.

Robin was silent a while.

'How is it that Mathew is here at all?' she asked. 'You said you hadn't met his mother, so you couldn't have brought him.'

'An old friend happened to be in London prior to the marriage. He offered to bring Mathew out here while they honeymooned, and the offer was accepted. It was planned for someone to return the boy, or the couple to collect him themselves. Then' ... a sigh ... 'this happened.' Tamar Warren spread his big cattleman hands. — And yet, Robin found herself thinking of those hands, he wasn't a cattleman, or at least he had become one only recently. Promotion had been his business. The study of it had taken him abroad for years.

That fact puzzled her. Surely if a man was inclined, as Jim had said, to the land and not business, he would have come here before.

'Yes?' asked Tamar Warren, and Robin gave a little guilty start.

'You were probing me, Miss Mansfield, what was it you wanted to know?'

'Why?' she asked. 'Why you have only come back now? Jim said you were keen.' — What Jim had actually said was: 'But here' ... Yarani ... 'was his heart.'

'My Grandfather Glenville was a shrewd old man,' Tamar said.

'Very shrewd.' Robin's voice was significant.

'We won't go into that,' the man dismissed. 'You see, I could offer a different interpretation. I could call him far-seeing, for instance, prudent.'

'I'll settle for acquisitive.'

'I said we wouldn't discuss it.'

'You also said your grandfather was shrewd.'

'Over me, I meant. He had seen the sheep topple.'

'They're on their feet again,' Robin pointed out.

'Seen fortunes lost on the land.' Tamar Warren ignored her. 'So he put me to business instead of the other. I had to complete my course, prove myself, before I could come back.'

'Which you did.'

'Thanks only to my father, who carried on all those years I was away, since Grandfather Glenville died soon after his decree.'

'Then the property hopped a generation and came to you?'

'My father was not a Glenville,' the man reminded her. 'Neither in name nor inclination. In fact, he loathed the land.'

'So does Jim,' came in Robin with interest. 'Ginny, too. It's funny, isn't it, how families split up.'

'My father wasn't family,' he reminded her again. 'He had no love for this place, only love for my mother, who died much too young, and after that for their child.'

Robin said, 'You,' and he nodded.

'Because of this love,' Tamar Warren went on, 'he stuck it out all those years, he kept the place for me. Do you wonder that I feel about him as I do? He's had a rotten life, Mother leaving him so early, Grandfather naturally being the king of his own domain. Then when I do take over at last and he goes to England and meets his Lilith, this thing happens.' Tamar Warren pressed one big fist into the palm of the other hand.

'You don't resent a stepmother?' Robin dared.

'My father was a lonely man for many years.'

'Then how do you feel about a stepbrother?' she asked slyly.

'I suspect you know already,' he replied bluntly.

'If I did I wouldn't be asking you. How do you react after all this time to a small brother?'

'Step.'

44

'Yes, Pab— Mathew said it was different from a step you stand on.'

'He's a funny young 'un. Well, Miss Mansfield, I'm neutral, neither jumping for joy nor cast down.'

'Mathew reported to me that you considered him a basement,' Robin said in mock innocence.

'Yes, I was embarrassed,' interpreted Tamar Warren with a grin. He shed years when he smiled, he looked almost a boy himself, his teeth gleamed white in his leather-dark face. He must have been continually in the sun since he had left his promotion business and returned to Yarani.

'Will you go over to England to see your father?' she asked seriously.

'I hope to, if there's time. But first of all the child must be settled. Unless he's happily fixed up I can't go, for I don't want anything to be taken away from my father's last days, and Lilith's unease, because of her son, could inflict that.'

Robin nodded, she followed his reasoning, but she still could not understand why *she* was so necessary.

'Do you have to know?' he came back when she inquired. 'Isn't your desire to stay on here as long as you can enough for you?'

'It will be, but I thought I'd still like to know. Is Pab— Mathew difficult or something, so that anyone else won't take him on?'

'No difficulty so far as I can see, but I have no house-keeper, Glenville is a strictly male household.'

'So is Mathew male.'

'But brought up entirely by a woman. He was the only child. Good heavens, Miss Mansfield, I'm not so obtuse that I can't see that the boy is out of his depth with me.'

'No,' Robin agreed, 'I saw it, too.'

'Yet well disguised,' admired the cattleman. 'He's a brave little fellow.'

'You could bring in a housekeeper,' Robin suggested.

'I could, and it did occur to me, and then the letter arrived.' At her lifting brows, he explained: 'From my father's wife, declining my offer to hold on to Mathew until – well, until it was all over. I can give you the wording. – "Thank you, Tamar, but I couldn't leave Mat with a household of men, also I couldn't leave him with a strange woman should you decide to employ one for that reason. It would be better for your father's comfort not to have my boy home yet, but I still couldn't allow it unless there was someone personal, someone intimate ... perhaps if you were married, for instance, or even intending to be ..." It went on in that strain.'

'Ah,' Robin said.

'So you see light at last?'

'Yes.'

'Does it make a difference?' he asked.

'I told you I would stay on, but I'm glad I know.'

'Your brother and his wife intend leaving at once,' Tamar Warren said presently. 'Mathew will move over immediately. Also I've asked my city agency for a woman.'

'That's not necessary,' protested Robin.

'Oh, I know Lilith doesn't want one, but you will.'

'I never have yet.'

'But Ginny has been doing the cooking, I gathered.'

... Ginny. He had got on to that very soon, Robin thought.

'Yes,' she nodded, 'but one adult! One little boy!'

'Is that all?'

'Oh, there's Wattie, but he does for himself.'

'Wattie?' he queried.

'Our handyman,' she explained.

'Then who is Ragsy?'

'Ragsy?' she murmured faintly.

'Mathew has mentioned a Ragsy.'

She flushed, and diverted: 'So you see a woman isn't at

46

all necessary, Mr. Warren.'

'All the same one is coming, not only because of you and Mathew, but because of Noel Levers.'

'And who is he?'

'He'll be managing my new property for me.' He saw her wince and said at once: 'I'm sorry.'

'It's all right. I have to get used to it.' She gulped. 'So you think a woman will be needed to cook for three?'

'Also to fit the propriety angle,' he added significantly. 'Noel is a very attractive young fellow.'

'Then perhaps I could be staying on at Nooroo indefinitely,' Robin said lightly to help dismiss the weight she had felt at that 'my new property'.

'No, I don't think so,' Warren said.

'He's married?'

A pause. Then. 'No. But I still don't think you would find Nooroo without you as boss quite to your liking.'

'Jim was the boss.'

'Not, I believe, that you would have noticed. Now, Miss Mansfield, don't explode, it was just "hear talk".'

'Then keep your hear talk to yourself, please.'

'I will. Also I'm sorry I spoke like that. I didn't mean that there'll be no meeting of eyes between you and Levers – good heavens, he's eligible enough, and you're quite attractive – but that any meeting with a view to Nooroo would be right out, because managers move round unless they happen to buy up, and when it comes to Nooroo—'

'What you have you'll hold?'

'Exactly.' He was looking between the leaves of the trees now. 'Your brother and sister have brought out a tray to the verandah and are obviously trying to penetrate the shadows. Shall we emerge from the shadows hand-in-hand?'

'We weren't sitting in the shadows.'

'No, you saw to that, didn't you? Yet we could still emerge hand-in-hand.' Before she could answer, could

47

decline, he captured her hand lightly yet inescapably in his. Together they returned to the house.

It did not take Ginny and Jim long to pack up. Ginny, apart from things she had actually needed, had never unpacked; Jim, although it had been his own place, had never really belonged. In fact there were more of Ginny's things to be carried out to the waggon, boxes she never had opened and was now taking back unopened, than for Jim. It was unbelievable, Robin thought, how anyone who, apart from school, had lived here all his life, could have accumulated so little. Most of what he had accumulated appeared to be expendable, for he was leaving the greater part of it behind. He looked at his sparse luggage with triumph and said: 'That's the way to travel.'

'And leave?' Robin could not help herself saying that.

'I'm sorry, Robbie, I guess I'm my mother all over again, as you are Grandfather. You were always "Me, too." Now I find I can't look back, only forward, especially since I have this job . . .'

That had hurried things along. A job, and a favourable one, awaited Jim. Tamar Warren had got it for him. She must remember just to say Tamar, Robin sighed, recalling the cattleman's last instruction.

'Ostensibly we're engaged, so you can't go around calling me Mr. Warren,' he had said.

'They used to once,' Robin pointed out. 'Even after they were married it was Mr. Smith, Mr Jones.'

'A century ago we moved on, didn't you know?'

'Oh, I know,' Robin had said tightly. She had been thinking that if it had been that century, Nooroo would still belong to the Mansfields. Even though the arrangement was a good one, good for Jim and his wife, good for her, there were times still that she could not bear it, could not face the fact of Nooroo changing hands.

But one had to live in the present . . . 'a century ago we

moved on, didn't you know?' . . . and for the present, anyway, she could still look out on golden fields, on distant blue hills, on *her* kind of place.

It seemed no time before her brother and sister were bidding final goodbyes, final since they had been saying them all the week. Jim was kissing her and mumbling: 'Try to understand, old thing, and you know where to come if you do come.'

For it was not 'when' now, but 'if'. Robin Mansfield and Tamar Warren had announced their engagement, and to prove it Robin wore a simple but pretty ring. When it came to Ginny's turn to bid goodbye, the girl stood hesitant a long moment. Several times during the busy week she had stood just that way, but nothing had evolved.

'Robbie,' she said now.

'Be happy, please, Ginny,' Robin wished hurriedly, for that hesitancy in Ginny had not escaped her; she felt there was something the girl wanted to tell her. Was it all off between Jim and Ginny, and would she learn later? Would they write to tell her?

'Robbie, I think you should know—' endeavoured Ginny.

'Yes, Ginny, but Jim looks about to blow the horn at any moment, and if there's anyone I despise it's the blower of a horn.'

'But—'

'Hurry, darling. Tell me next time.'

'Next time,' said Ginny, half hesitated again, then shrugged, kissed Robin and ran down to the waiting car.

I know what all that was about Robin thought sadly. Well, let's hope that the city that they both prefer will give them second thoughts.

She herself had no time for any thoughts. The same day as her brother and sister departed, Mathew arrived. Tamar fetched him along with his small bags, and while

Robin unpacked for him, he sat on the verandah looking out on the fields.

He was still there when Robin came out. Though he only sat as any visitor would sit, to her he seemed a squire gazing out on his possessions.

'The landlord counting his gold,' she said lightly ... but with an intentional sting in it.

'Is there any?'

'The fleece is turning that colour again.'

'Yes, but Nooroo's flocks have been considerably reduced, haven't they?'

'They can be built up.'

'Which I intend doing. But I will not be in any competition for the biggest numbers. I intend mainly to experiment here. I thought of trying a variety of things. I'm even considering sunflowers.'

'I thought of them, too,' Robin said eagerly.

'Great minds,' he commented lightly. 'Also a small stud. I've always been keen on horses.'

'Who isn't?'

'You mean you wouldn't be against one?' he said as eagerly as she had agreed eagerly to those sunflowers. She looked at him in surprise.

'Would it matter if I was?'

That dashed him. She could not help feeling sorry for his dampened look. He had been so lit up.

'I didn't mean it like that,' she proffered, 'at least I didn't mean any discouragement. I really meant – well, is this the right district?'

'This is to be discovered. Oh, I know for perfect breeding you want soft rain and limestone, but even if we only breed our own requirements ... perhaps some material for the provincial races ... it could be profitable as well as pleasurable. How are you when it comes to acting midwife to a mare?'

'I've brought a few calves to the light of day,' Robin admitted, 'and I was around when Ribbons came, so I

50

guess a mare would be all right.'

'It's an idea, anyway. Also, I plan a small afforestation, it would have to be small with our touchy rainfall.'

'No cotton? No rice?'

'I'm not promising, just considering a mixed bag.' He got up from his chair. 'Kid settled in?'

'I believe he will.'

'You'll have a few days together to jell, then the house-keeper and Levers will come.'

'In that order, of course,' Robin said primly.

'Of course.' He disregarded her sly note. 'Will you fix up rooms?'

'Yes, Mr. Warren,' she agreed, and, because there was no one around to raise brows at 'Mr. Warren' instead of 'Tamar,' he nodded back, and left.

Robin went in to see Mathew. He had placed his few books around, his favourite matchbox toys. When you came upon him unexpectedly, you surprised that little droop in him. He was, as Tamar had said, a brave little fellow. Well, he was going to get all the help he could from her, she determined.

Robin went out of her way to amuse him, include him, and on the third day she was rewarded.

'I like you, Ragsy,' he said. They had come to an agreement of Ragsy and Pablo strictly between themselves.

'I like you, Pablo.'

'You're 'zackly the same as my mother,' Mathew awarded, 'except you're different.'

Robin nodded gravely.

'You have the same faces,' Mathew resumed, 'except she doesn't look like you.'

'How interesting,' Robin now murmured.

'The zack same hair except she's dark and you're — What are you, Ragsy?'

'Just a kind-of, I think.'

'Kind of brown, kind of white, kind of yellow?' he asked.

'Yes, darling. The sun does it.'

'Will it do it for me?'

'Would you like that?'

'I like everything you have, Ragsy, because it's just like my mother except different. Here's someone coming.' He looked out at the peppercorn drive at an approaching car.

Robin looked, too, seeing at the same time that Mathew had not brought in from the garden The Honourable Member. It had been his turn to have a loan of The Honourable Member from school, since for some inexplicable reason the battered golliwog from the toy cupboard was very popular, and had to be strictly doled out for his nightly cuddles and loves. He had become The Honourable Member when one day Robin had given a practical lesson on Parliament, and had chosen Golly at random for a parliamentary figure. He was one of those stuffed morsels that children take to immediately, ignoring costlier toys. They had discarded her Prime Minister and Leader of the Opposition, but vied with each other for the Honourable Member, allotting all sorts of names, according to their ages, to it, from The Abominable Ember to Abdominal December. Miriam, a romantic even at nine, generally called the battered golly D'You Remember.

Mathew, having his turn to keep golly overnight, had taken The Honourable Member out to show Wattie, explain about him, and must have left him by the flower bed that Wattie had been weeding. Well, it was too late to run out and pick him up now, for by now the car, a hire car from the village, was pulling up, and the passenger, female variety, was getting out.

She was not a local, that was the first thing that Robin registered. The second was that she was little older than Robin herself. They had so few callers out here that Robin should have guessed her purpose at once, but years of looking after themselves had preserved for Robin a strict picture of what housekeepers were like, and that was kindly, capable and inclined to be comfortably plump. This young woman was none of these, so Robin did not guess.

One thing, she thought rather with relief, she hasn't any bag, so she can't be a saleslady and she can't intend stopping. For somehow she did not like the young woman, though she must not let Mathew sense her antipathy.

Mathew, however, saw things for himself. He looked at the new arrival with a distaste that grew to an active dislike, when, instead of stepping over The Honourable Member in her path, she kicked him aside.

'She kicked The Honourable Member!' Mathew was one of the few who got the name right.

'Darling, he was in her way, and he's only an old golly.'

'Only an old golly! Who is she, Ragsy?'

'Probably selling something.'

'Don't buy it, then.'

Robin, who at that moment could not have bought anything since her employment to Jim had ceased, and the employment to Tamar Warren only begun, remonstrated halfheartedly. She saw, and was pleased, that the hire car was waiting.

Even though the meter was ticking up the cents, the girl took her time. She looked the house up and down, looked out to the fields, looked to the barns. Then she came to the verandah where Robin and Mathew stood.

'I'll see the room,' she announced.

'The room?'

'I'm the housekeeper ... that is, of course, if it suits me.'

'Oh – oh, of course. It's not ready yet, though.'

'Neither am I, but I'll see it.' The girl stepped out, so Robin did, too. She led her to one of the rooms.

'Humph,' the young woman said, looking up and down

the same as she had outside.

'Will it—'

'Yes, it will do. I can always change it around and spread myself.' She now looked at Robin. 'You would be the Mansfield girl who's staying on.'

Tamar Warren must have briefed her, Robin thought a little angrily. She said she was.

'Until you marry, I believe. I'd never do that. I'd never wait. I don't believe in water running under the bridge.' She stared at Robin with impertinent curiosity, and Robin knew that she must have reddened from the warmth she felt in her cheeks.

The girl laughed to herself, said she would start next Monday and that meanwhile she was going on to Westerfield for a few days. Westerfield was further along the line.

'When I start next week I'll tell you how I want things done,' she announced coolly.

Robin summoned enough daring to ask: 'Isn't it you who'll be doing them?'

'My own corner only, Miss Mansfield, and I'll have no interference, and no' . . . a glance at Mathew standing belligerently by . . . 'pests.'

'We go to school three days a week.'

'So I hear.' – Tamar, Robin thought, had said a lot to this person.

The hire car man tooted his horn, and the young woman called 'Coming!' To Robin and Mathew she tossed, 'See you,' and went down the hall, down the steps and across to the car. The car reversed and ran between the pepper trees again to the road.

'I don't like her,' Mathew said flatly.

Robin said nothing, for if she had spoken she would have had to agree with him, which wouldn't have been the right thing at all. For she did not like her, either.

CHAPTER FOUR

HER lack of enthusiasm over the new housekeeper did not bother Robin. She decided simply that the young woman would not be suitable, so therefore there was no problem. She might have had doubts as to how Tamar Warren would have reacted if the complaint had been solely on her behalf, but any doubt in Mathew, she knew, would never be disregarded by that man. She had only to say to Tamar that his little stepbrother would not be happy with the applicant, and a new arrangement would be made.

'She was awful,' Mathew said later. 'If I thought she was coming, Ragsy, I would—'

'She wasn't awful, she isn't coming, so you won't,' smiled Robin.

But that evening, Mathew fortunately out of earshot, Robin learned differently.

Their particular phone signal went, and Robin picked up the receiver. The cattleman had evidently decided that at this time of evening there would be no one listening, or alternatively if they happened to listen that they would not connect the pair of them, for he inquired formally: 'Miss Mansfield?'

'Yes.'

'My father is worse.'

'Oh ... I'm sorry.' How inadequate, Robin thought wretchedly, are words.

'I'm wondering how the position is, whether I could get away at once. I know it's short time for you to judge Pat' ... so Pat was the young woman's name; the same as with Ginny, Mr. Tamar Warren had picked that up at once ... 'but if at all possible, I mean if Mathew was amenable, it would be what I want.'

Of course he would want it. Now Robin's heart went out to him in his unhappy position.

But – Pat?

'How did the interview go?' he asked urgently.

'Oh – briefly.' It was all Robin could think to say.

'Yes, she said she was going on to some friends. She seemed all right ... it's hard, of course, over a phone.'

'You didn't meet her then?'

'No. What's she like?'

'Young.' Well, what more could you say? If he asked for details, which, seeing the amount of details he had given to this Pat he probably would, then she would give them to him.

But he didn't. He said eagerly: 'Then I could get away?'

She hesitated only the briefest of seconds, but he caught the hesitation.

'Are you unsure?' he probed.

'No. No, of course not. Go by all means. I was just looking out to see where Mathew had gone.'

'Don't fuss. Don't "dust" him. By the sound of Pat, she'll be good for the young fellow. Brisk and crisp, just what a kid like Mathew needs.'

'Yes,' said Robin faintly.

'Anyway, I want things settled,' he went on. 'Noel arrives the end of the week, so whoever eventually comes must be established by then.'

'That propriety?' she asked primly.

'We're country, remember,' he defended.

'I remember.'

'Then it's all right?'

'All right.'

'Thank you, you've taken a load off my mind.'

Robin said nothing; you could not wish a happy journey, any of the usual sort of things, not on this occasion. 'Goodbye, Mr. Warren,' she said instead.

56

'Goodbye,' he said, and rang off.

At school the next day one of the mothers soothed over-extravagantly, 'Never mind, dear, days pass, you'll soon have your man back again,' and Robin knew by this that Tamar had actually left. She also knew she would have to prepare Mathew for Monday's unwelcome addition.

'Her,' said Mathew when she did.

'Pat, not her. And Pablo, Tamar had to get away so he could see his sick father. You knew his father was sick, didn't you?'

'Yes, that's why I'm here,' the little boy said bleakly.

'If I'd told Tamar what I would ordinarily have told him, about us not particularly caring for Pat, I mean, he would have delayed going, and perhaps never have seen his dad.' Mathew was an exceptional little boy, Robin thought as she said it; you did not speak down to him, you told him the truth.

'All right,' he accepted, 'but I won't bring The Honourable Member home any more, not after her kicking him.'

'No. I wouldn't. Anyway, it's Ellen's turn.'

Ellen. As she said the name, Robin barely stopped a sigh. If you could term a little school a diamond, and anything to do with children had certain diamond properties, then Ellen was the flaw. An unco-operative ten-year-old, whatever Ellen gave her attention to, there instantly sprang trouble. Crayons got crushed ... intentionally under Ellen's shoe, Robin always suspected ... pages disappeared from books, ink spilled, lunches were either missing or messed up.

She was not a country child. Neither were her parents, the Crokers, country. They had arrived only several weeks ago at Yarani and were supposedly share-farming out at Doughboy, ten miles west of town. Report had it that Mallison, the other sharer, wasn't too pleased with his partner.

Robin wasn't pleased, either. Ellen, apart from the first week of enrolment, had never been paid for. You couldn't dislike a child for that, she knew, in fact you couldn't dislike a child, full stop, but if you *could* ... well, she could Ellen.

'It is not *so* Ellen's turn,' pointed out Mathew fairly.

'Ellen says it is,' said Robin. As always with the arrogant, she thought, too, you give way to them, take the line of least resistance.

She thought that again the next day as she handed Ellen the golly to take home.

'He's pretty moth-eaten,' patronized Ellen, and one fingernail probed at a loose eye. By the time The Honourable Member comes back he'll have only one eye, thought Robin.

'You're getting a cook,' said Ellen next.

'How did you learn that?'

'We know her.'

'From when you were in Sydney?'

'Ask no questions and you'll be told no lies,' said Ellen parrot-wise; evidently it had been said to her, but it did not remove any of the deliberate impertinence.

'I know what you have in your desk,' Ellen said next.

That shocked ... yet actually did not surprise ... Robin; you would have had to have eyes at the back of your head to supervise Ellen's sharp little eyes. But still the girl's cool announcement was distasteful, since weapons themselves were distasteful, and to think this child knew ...

'You're a busybody,' she said sharply.

'I'll tell my dad on you,' Ellen retaliated.

'Do.'

'My mum, too.'

Robin took a deep breath, then counted ten. After all, it would be foolish to mark this as an incident by showing any interest.

'Bring The Honourable Member back tomorrow, dear.'

'He looks sick,' said Ellen, 'he might even be dead by then.'

The best way was to ignore her, Robin decided. But she felt they had seen the last of Golly.

Pat ... Robin had not found out her name ... arrived on the Monday. Previously Robin had determined to make their mutual stay at Nooroo as amicable as possible, however hard it proved, but one look at Pat told Robin that she in her turn had made no such determination. Well, it took two, Robin thought, and if only for Pablo's sake I'll turn the other cheek.

However, if by no means friendly, the girl did not go out of her way to be disagreeable, in fact she seemed not to want to bother with either of them, which suited Robin. She decided that if she kept Pablo from under Pat's feet and put up with things that would ordinarily have angered her, they might last out the short time they both would be required here.

Mathew was her weak point; like all children he was here, there and everywhere, and Pat wanted him nowhere that she happened to be

'Keep the kid away!' she snapped to Robin.

The unfairness of it snapped something in Robin, and her determination faltered a little.

'He's as much right here as we have.'

'I have the right of my position,' said Pat. 'I don't know about you, though of course you're engaged to Warren, aren't you' ... a slyness there? ... 'but I have a job to do, and that brat hasn't.'

'He's Tamar Warren's brother.'

'Stepbrother. And I don't care if he's his bosom pal, I won't have him round me.'

If she had been a good cook, Robin would have put it down to temperament, but the food was just food. Robin ate it, tasted a vast difference from Ginny's offerings, but still accepted it. Pablo was inclined to push it aside had not Robin kicked him under the table each time.

'What a horror!' Pat said of the little boy.

'Not really, he—' But Robin decided not to argue. She could not stop herself remarking, though, that Pat obviously did not care for children.

'I loathe them. How you stand that kid around you is beyond me.'

'And yet,' came in Robin smoothly, 'you're a friend of Ellen Croker's.'

Pat stopped what she was doing and gave Robin a quick suspicious look. But she said nothing.

'Ellen Croker,' Robin repeated. 'She comes to the school.' As Pat still did not speak, she went on, 'She mentioned you.'

'Little stickynose,' said Pat at last. 'All kids are monsters.'

If Ellen, who was a friend, or a child of a friend, was a monster, then Robin wisely decided she had better keep the little boy, who was no friend, away from the house as much as she could. It was not hard to do, he loved Pat no more than she loved him, and he adored the outdoors. He and Robin spent hours in the paddocks. She taught him to ride. She took him to the billabong to see the water birds swooping over the trapped river after gnats, their sudden descents and triumphant ascents making flight patterns in the gold shimmery air. She demonstrated to him the best way to boil a billy, make a damper, with the help of the two kelpies round up a flock of sheep. She showed him the pleasure of caring for living things, the fun of spreading hay, the reward of releasing wire-entrapped cows, the sadness turned to joy after a ewe died, but Wattie performed a quick caesarean and you heard a new soft bleat. She made him sniff the good smell of wool. Wattie gave him milking lessons, he was allowed to set down a batch of eggs for chickens.

The only flaw in his little life, apart, of course, from being away from his mother, was the non-return, as Robin had anticipated, by Ellen of The Honourable

Member, but then, children being resilient little people, he, and the rest of the class, duly recovered, particularly when Ellen, whom none of them had liked, never came back, either. She did not speak of this to Pat and Pat said nothing to her, though Robin knew the cook spoke regularly over the phone to the Crokers.

One of Yarani's rare social gatherings was approaching, every year the village put on a fête. Robin asked Mathew if he liked fêtes.

'I don't know them,' he said.

'Lots of fun, darling – coconut shies, wishing wells, hurdy-gurdies.'

'They're fairs,' Mathew informed her reproachfully.

'This will be a fair, then. Will we go?'

'Will there be maypoles?'

'No.'

'Morris dancing?'

'No.'

'Oh,' said Mathew dubiously.

Robin said there would be rodeo riding, and the little boy conceded that it should be exciting, though it wouldn't be a real fair, Ragsy. Fairs were on village commons, and Yarani had none.

'Is *she* coming?'

'Pat? I don't know. But we'll go together.'

'Just the two of us,' he agreed.

But *three* went, and Mathew was quite pleased about that, for at once he took to Noel Levers, who arrived several days later, and was an immediate success with the little boy. As for Robin, she, too, found she could not help herself warming to the young man.

She had thought she would feel resentful, suffer a pang at every innovation Noel proposed. But Noel conferred with her over every item, and when at last she protested half laughing, half crying, 'Oh, Noel' . . . for it had been Noel and Robin at once . . . 'you know you don't need to,' he had said:

'But I do need, Robin, and I must. It's your place.'

'It isn't really, you know.'

'Oh, yes, I'm aware of that, but I still feel it's yours, somehow.' He was tall, fair, clear-eyed, quite charming in an unaware way. 'Somehow I feel it's going to remain yours,' he said.

What I have I hold, Robin thought of Tamar Warren, and she shook her head ruefully. 'It isn't possible, but all the same, has anyone ever told you that you're very nice?'

'I'll have to think, Robin,' he smiled, 'but I can answer without thinking for your housekeeper; *she* doesn't like me at all.'

'Not my housekeeper, Mr. Warren's.' Robin remembered the situation and corrected: 'Tamar's.'

'Isn't it the same?' he smiled teasingly.

A little uneasily Robin went on, 'Tamar insisted on a housekeeper for conventional reasons – imagine that in the nineteen-seventies!'

'Country towns are either one way or another,' Noel smiled reasonably. 'What is Yarani? Avant-garde, or otherwise?

'Do you know what,' Robin giggled, 'I don't believe I can answer that.'

'I think you've had your head in the lucerne all these years.'

'Could be. I'm strictly a station, not village, girl. You said Pat didn't like you?'

'She gave me a first quick scrutiny, then put me definitely aside.'

'Yes, she does that. But it was different with Mathew with you, wasn't it?'

Noel gave his wide smile. 'He's a bonzer kid,' he said.

'He thinks you're bonzer, too, he's taken to you much quicker than he took to Mr. – to Tamar.'

'Any news from the boss?'

'No. I was just going to say no news is good news, but

then it can't be, not there, can it?' Robin's voice became grave.

'A damn shame,' said Noel. 'I only hope it's an easy release for Warren Senior and that Tamar makes it in time.'

'One thing,' said Robin more brightly, 'Mathew has settled down since you came. He had accepted me, but there was none of the blissful contentment that there is now. He was missing his mother abominably.'

'To have such a kid as he is she would have to be missed. I think she must be a very lovely person.'

'Special, Tamar anticipated.'

'Well, he's met her now and can judge. – Hi, Mat, want to ride out to the western paddock with me? A lamb was dropped this afternoon and I'm bringing him in for your special care because his mother isn't up to it. Robin will show you how to feed him from a bottle. You call a lamb like that a poddy.'

Did Mathew want to go, smiled Robin watching him beat Noel to the horses, just did he?

Pat gave an amused smile when Robin asked her if she would be going to the fair ... Robin, too, was calling it a fair now.

'Not likely,' the girl said with contempt.

'It's fun.'

'For yokels.'

Robin let that pass, but she made a show of concern by asking Pat if she would be all right left by herself.

'Because,' she explained, 'even Wattie goes. It's the same right through Yarani. Fair Day is Down Tools Day. Simply everybody goes.' As she said it she wondered had *he* been here would Tamar Warren have gone; he definitely did not seem the fair type.

Almost as though she had read the location of her thoughts, Pat said:

'All Glenville, too?'

'Everybody,' Robin repeated. She asked again if Pat would be all right.

'Of course. Have a good time,' Pat wished carelessly. 'Also, if the kid comes back sick from too much fairy floss keep him out of my kitchen.'

'I'll look after him,' Robin assured her.

'Well, one thing, I won't.'

The fair morning dawned bright and slightly breezy, breezes were something that didn't happen much in Parani, the hot nor'-west usually went in for still shimmery weather. The wind, Robin thought, should please the organizers; the flags would flutter where they usually hung limp.

Noel brought round the car and Mathew sat beside him and Robin at the back, a seating that suited Robin but evidently faintly amused Pat, who came out to see them go. She smiled contemptuously, but just as they started off she called anxiously: 'What about the old man?'

'Wattie went with the Lewis crowd,' called back Robin. She said to Noel as they went down the peppercorn drive that that was kind of Pat anyhow, not wanting the handyman to miss out.

'I don't know,' was Noel's rather cryptic reply.

'What do you mean, Noel?'

'Nothing, of course.'

A mile further on, Noel said, 'I don't think Edwards should have let all Glenville go.'

'But which member could you deprive?'

'He could have rostered them as to which hour and how long duration. However, it's his concern, not mine. Also' . . . shrugging . . . 'when it comes to it I haven't done that, either. – Look, Mathew, there's a rodeo float ahead.'

Mathew looked at it in fascination; it was one of the outfits that do the country towns, and it bore the intriguing name of Rough Riders. They passed it carefully,

Mathew waving enthusiastically to the driver.

'There's another one,' the boy called, pointing ahead. This time the rodeo truck was named 'Hit The Dirt.'

In Yarani village the procession introducing the fair was already in progress. For a small place it was quite a large one, beginning with a Cobb & Co, then after that with anyone interested enough to dress up, dress up their car, bike or lorry, and march, or drive, by.

Parade over, they hurried to the cricket ground where a small band was trying to get heard over voices shouting over loudspeakers, shouting through megaphones and simply shouting.

With Mathew between them, they did the fair rounds, the same as all fairs whether they are set on village greens or far west cricket grounds, Robin thought – the same food tents, drink tents, merry-go-rounds, shies and chocolate wheels to entice them.

Mathew enjoyed it, but he kept on looking anxiously at the arena and the corral in case the rough riders started without him. Finally the oldies took pity on him and found a good seat and stopped there. A wood-chopping contest was going on behind the corral, but Mathew could not be budged. He was looking wide-eyed at the riders waiting to begin, wearing their ten-gallon hats and brightly checked shirts.

Then it was on. Men with strong boomerang legs were coming out one after the other from the corral, sitting long in the saddle, every nerve tense. The offsiders in the arena were making split-second leaps for safety as horses thundered by, as roping, drafting and roughriding were performed.

Mathew never moved, never uttered a word, and Robin did not wonder. There was no more virile a scene, she thought, than a lean, hard-riding, rough man disciplining, or trying to discipline, flying hooves as fresh horses pig-rooted, kicked and bucked.

At lunch Mathew still said nothing, ate little. All the

better, deemed Robin wisely, when a child is so excited.

But for all his thrall when finally it was over, Mathew only allotted sparse praise.

'Good, darling?' Robin asked.

'Yes.'

'As good as Morris dancing?'

After some thought Mathew awarded: 'Yes.'

They stopped in town ... if one store, one hotel, one garage, one post office-bank was that, and all the fair-goers paused on their rounds to talk. Robin introduced Noel to everyone who came across to her, and that, she told Noel, was the entire population.

'Not Pat,' he said a little oddly.

'Well, you know what I mean, Noel. Possibly a few people aren't here. I know the Crokers aren't, for instance, for I would have noticed Ellen.'

When Bert Mallison, share-farming with the Crokers, came up to Robin, she learned why she had not seen them, why Ellen had not been at school this week.

'They're left,' Bert said.

'Where?'

'Look, I'm not trying to find out, I'm just too relieved to be free of them. I don't think any of Yarani will fret.'

Yarani didn't fret ... but later it wondered, wondered if the Crokers' move had anything to do with a lot of other things that had been moved.

It was one of the Glenville men who first discovered the thefts. Returning to Glenville to change for the dance that was to be put on that night, he retraced his steps at once to report some bad news. His digs, and all the others he had promptly peered into, had been turned upside down. The homestead had been ransacked.

Glenville was the start of a formidable list of losses. Practically every homestead reported tools, equipment, clothes, in many instances money, missing. The fact of the fair, which everyone had attended, made it easy, if unpalatable, to understand the robberies. While Yarani

66

had played, the snatches had been made. As Nooroo was the furthest out, no one knew as yet, but old Wattie was apprehensive.

The handyman sought out Robin to tell her about the little hoard he kept in his room. 'I don't bank,' he said, 'I don't get into town, and anyway, I don't believe in them banks.'

'You'll be all right, Wattie. Pat was staying home, remember.'

'That's what I thought, Miss Robbie.'

'What do you mean, Wattie?'

'She was a friend of the Crokers, and they've gone. Very funny, I reckon, leaving just a few days before we were all to be away for the day. And leaving for where? How far away? Just out of the town, you reckon? Nice and handy?'

'Oh, Wattie, you're thinking the worst. Your money's all right. Pat stayed at Nooroo and she would guard it.'

Only when they got home the girl was not there.

Neither were a lot of things. Wattie's hoard was gone, some loose money of Noel's, all that he had not taken with him, a watch of Robin's, even a piggy bank of Mathew's.

'Pat—' disbelieved Robin.

'Yes, Rob,' Noel said. 'And I have to admit now I had a feeling all along. I was a fool not to speak out, but new to the place, not knowing the girl ... Well, I guess I never will know her now.'

'You mean she went intentionally?'

'Yes.'

'But you don't think she planned all this?'

'I do think. And what a golden opportunity, Rob – the entire district at a fair.'

'But she couldn't have done it alone,' protested Robin.

She could have done it with the Crokers.'

'You don't think ...'

Again Noel said: 'I think.' He went on: 'I believe it was planned like this some time ago. If you followed these things as I happen to have followed them you would find a long police record on robberies done during local functions. I think the Croker crowd have had the situation well in hand for some time, I think this isn't the first by any means.'

'How did Glenville fare?' Robin asked.

'Badly. The entire station was a shambles. I wouldn't like to be in Edwards' shoes when the boss gets back – he should have left someone in the place.' Noel had the humility to add, 'Even though I didn't.'

'What are the chances of any recovery, Noel?'

'Going by previous instances, they . . . our thieves . . . could be right away by now. No, I think we can all put it down to bitter experience. The Crokers would have dug in somewhere when they left the share farm, somewhere strategic, and the moment we all got out Pat would have given the signal and then the lot of them joined forces in a quick and telling swoop.'

'They can't hope to get away with it,' Robin scorned.

'They have before.'

'Not all the time. I really meant they can't always be lucky.'

'No, but it is our time we're concerned about, isn't it? Poor old Watt.'

'Poor everybody,' sighed Robin. She added: 'The wretches, if only they could be found.'

. . . They were found . . . and through none other than The Honourable Member! Although Robin had no doubt that Ellen never had cared about the battered golliwog, evidently she must have had a sense of acquisition like her parents, for when they had all finally left with their spoils, the stuffed golly had left, too.

But somewhere along a country sidetrack the golly had either fallen or been thrown out of the truck. Knowing Ellen, Robin knew that the throwing out could have fitted in with a mood of spitefulness.

The toy found by an astute policeman had been a route indication. Detectives sent up from Ranley had come upon the group hidden in a thicket by a creek sorting through their spoils for quick valuation, in some cases disposal, so as to travel lighter the next morning.

But the only travelling they did was into custody. Everyone was pleased at the prompt ending, Robin especially pleased for old Wattie ... *and then all at once sickeningly concerned for herself.*

For slowly and painfully she was piecing a few things together, and suddenly for some hateful reason she was remembering Ellen and Ellen saying: 'I know what you have in your desk.'

Is, Robin thought, *is it still there?*

She could not check at once because she had Mathew, but she knew every second would be a misery until she did find out. She thought about phoning the police, confiding in them, but when Noel came in to report further developments he seemed a kindlier source, and she fairly threw herself at him and tried to babble out her fears.

'There, there,' Noel soothed, 'there, old girl, start from the beginning again, you're not making sense' ... and over her head he smiled and nodded to someone who had just walked in.

'It's not as it looks,' he assured her easily. 'Rob's upset. We've all been that.'

'So I hear.' Her face crushed in Noel's lapel, Robin heard Tamar Warren's slow rather drawling tone.

She withdrew from Noel and turned to the man who had just entered. He did not look back at her.

'To be brief and to save questions,' Tamar said shortly, 'I made it over there in time. My father died several hours after I arrived. I came straight back.' He paused. 'Lilith will come later for Mathew.' Another pause. 'Spare me your episode details just now, please. I'm dead

69

on my feet, as you can imagine. You may resume your comforting, Noel.' A brief nod to his manager, but still none, Robin noted, to her.

He turned and went.

CHAPTER FIVE

TAMAR'S unexpected appearance had halted any desire in Robin to confide in Noel, tell him her fears, ask for his help and advice. When Tamar Warren had come in she had withdrawn from the manager, and now that he had gone she still stood away, even though Noel smiled warmly across at her and encouraged, 'What was it, Rob?'

'Nothing. Just—'

'I know, old girl. It's been one heck of a day. Evidently the same for poor Tamar, for he's not worrying about convention now, is he, only about physical rest. Which, incidentally, if you're equally unconcerned, Rob, I'll seek, too.'

'How could I be concerned?' she made herself grin. 'I've another male in the house, remember.'

'And completely tuckered, I'd say – I do believe that kid rode every rodeo event at the fair.'

'Yes, and now he has flaked out.'

'You do the same,' advised Noel, 'you look like the end of a day.'

She felt like the end of a thousand years, but as she got ready for bed she knew there would be little sleep for her that night. If she could have, she would have gone out to the schoolhouse at once, not wait for the morning, but old Wattie watched their stables like a hawk, even at night he could be depended on to sleep with one listening ear, and Noel saw to the locking up of the cars, and he was more than thorough. So it would have to be tomorrow. She slipped between the sheets and resigned herself to long hours of restlessness.

She must have slept some time, however, even if fitfully, for turning fretfully she opened her eyes and saw that morning had come, a grey unpromising morning, a most unusual morning for the west where even in winter the skies were a clear, if cold, bright blue. She looked now at the black streamers of clouds and wondered what the farmers were thinking of them. Rain was needed, out west rain always was needed, but steady, regular rain, not a furied outburst like that piling sky was threatening. Deluges could be catastrophic around Yarani, stormy creeks could run bankers, stream become raging rivers sometimes a mile wide. Because she had seen it all before, Robin barely prevented a little shiver, but, telling herself to be sensible, she turned her back on the ominous window and dressed.

It was a school morning, but it was obvious that no parent would send a child for classes today. Robin did not know whether to be pleased or sorry about that, she could certainly check quicker and safer without any child hindrance, but on the other hand having to open school would have been her excuse to be there to do what had to be done.

She rang Mrs. Gillespie and was answered by a surprised No, of course the kids wouldn't attend, hadn't Robin seen the sky? She rang several others and had the same reply. The rest rang her and said that Trevor or Michael or Miranda would not be in.

'Something's blowing up,' said the last parent. 'Bill's not at all happy.'

Well, blow up or not, an unhappy farmer or not, Robin knew that she had to get out to the schoolhouse to do some vital checking. Mathew was her worry, she could not take him with her on a morning like this, and Wattie would be running round under Noel's orders straightening and strengthening things to withstand whatever might be forthcoming.

Then providence arrived with Noel, who slept in an annexe and had his own phone switch, coming in and saying: 'Rob, the boss rang for me to go over to Glenville.

72

It's about instructions in case we're really in for something bad. I'm to take Mathew for the day. Some personal messages to pass on from his mum. You can come, too, if you like.'

'Is that from Mr. – from Tamar, too?' asked Robin suspiciously.

'Well—' evaded Noel, then grinned. 'But of course he intended to say that.'

'I'm sure he did, Noel, but I have a lot to do here.'

'Then I'll push off while the weather is still holding. You'll be all right, won't you?'

'Of course.'

The manager and the little boy went down the peppercorn drive, then turned in the direction of neighbouring Glenville, and Robin came back from the verandah where she had watched them off ... though checked that they did go would have been a more pertinent word ... then wondered what excuse she could make to Wattie for taking out the jeep. She had no need for any excuse, actually, he was only the handyman, but Wattie was an extremely conscientious old fellow. Robin had no doubt he already had put Noel in his place, and would not hesitate later, should he consider he needed it, to do the same with Tamar. She knew he always did it with her. Still, even if Wattie disapproved, she still had to get over to the school.

She went across to the garages.

There she found Wattie underneath their only other vehicle. She knelt down by him and asked what was wrong.

'Everything's wrong, durn thing won't go. I wanted to run out to check the western fence, if it blows hard it'll blow it with it, but the fool thing won't tick over.'

Robin, though she had other ideas as to the use of the jeep, tried her hand, too. It was to no avail, the engine was dead.

Dismayed, but trying not to show it, she left Wattie still

grumbling and still tinkering, and came out of the garages again.

It had begun to rain at last, only the slightest sound of little feet on the iron roof as yet, almost a mist, but still the drops had started.

By the time she regained the house again, though, the drops could be *felt*. The sky was dark now, not just ragged streamers of steely blue but solid black slabs. The rain was increasing at a quite alarming rate.

Once in the homestead she crossed to close the windows to stop the billowing curtains, but it was too late to prevent flying papers and strewn flowers. By the time she had righted them a thousand demons seemed to have been let loose outside the house, smashing demons of drops hitting down with such force that they bounced back again, and if you put out your hand to feel cutting viciously at you like small stilettos.

Robin had put out her hand and she withdrew it at once. She knew she could not possibly take Ribbons out in weather like this, and it would have to be the filly, seeing there was no car available.

She brewed a pot of tea, then, seeing a slight break in the downpour, took one across to Wattie. He was still under the jeep and he called out to her to leave the pot there and he would come out soon. When she emerged again the furied spurts of rain had slackened altogether, but no one looking at that sky could have thought the break would be for long. Even a newchum would have known that the elements were just getting their second wind, as it were, and Robin was no newchum. Yet *still*, she knew, she had to go across to the schoolhouse and find out.

She wasted no time in getting into slacks and windcheater. She ran over to the stables. No need to avoid Wattie, he would still be under the jeep. She saddled a plainly puzzled Ribbons, who was obviously as conscious of the weather as she was, then led the unwilling filly out of the barn. Just in case Wattie had emerged for his tea, Robin took the back way to the drive, led Ribbons some distance from the homestead before she mounted, then, out of view of the garages, she shoved her feet in the stirrups and gave Ribbons a little slap. The filly grunted as though to say, 'If you want to be an idiot, I suppose I have to be, too,' and got on with the job.

It was anything but a pleasant ride. The rain had fallen only briefly, but it had fallen intensely. The drive was as slippery as ice. The drops from the laden peppercorns, too, seemed to concentrate on the gap between Robin's neck and Robin's collar, so that icy streams kept rolling down her spine.

When they reached the road and took the side road in the school direction, mud had already formed in the deep corrugations, and what was not mire yet was as hazardous as an ice rink for poor Ribbons. If they were not sliding, they were squelching, and halfway there the cessation that had urged Robin to get the job over broke, and the rain, only a hundred times heavier, began again.

Robin was soaked in several minutes. No jacket in the world could have kept out that rain. Ribbons streamed water as though she was under a tap. It was a nightmare, and you could have called it night, too, thought Robin; it was so dark now you could barely see more than a few yards ahead.

There was a slight gutter, Robin knew, just before the schoolhouse, and she anticipated a little trouble there. Not much, though, she estimated hopefully; it was barely an indentation, her grandfather always had called these natural run-offs Irish drains. She judged that some water would have congregated, but probably only a little.

But she found she was wrong. Very wrong. Even alarmingly wrong. Yet still in her anxiety to get the thing finished she refused to believe that the gutter had actually grown to that fierce channel that confronted her.

When Ribbons hung back, Robin should have had the

country sense to pick up the filly's message; animals know danger before humans do. But she had to check that drawer, *she had to,* it was now the most important thing in the world to Robin, so when Ribbons got to the edge of the now considerable indentation, then stopped, she forced her girl on.

Ribbons whickered a protest, but Robin smacked the filly lightly and shouted: 'On. *On!'*

The filly plodded on with obvious difficulty; each step was an act of sheer hard toil, for she was probably trying to move through mud, but when Robin peered down to check she could see no further than her hand in the thick lashing rain.

Then Ribbons stepped deeper still, possibly into a more defined rut a rut with clay mud, sticky clinging mud, for the filly could not remove her hoof.

Robin called: 'Try – pull! Please, darling.' The hoof remained there.

Sliding off into the water, and going deeper than she cared about, Robin delved into the wretched mire and struggled, too. Ribbons took some moving, but eventually whatever was sucking her down loosened its grasp, and the foot moved.

Moved just at the same time as a wall of water moved towards Robin and the filly. The foolish thing about it, Robin thought stupidly, was that it seemed to be moving quite slowly, even deliberately, but that would be only illusion, she knew, the slow effect would be because with every inch it was gathering strength and body. It was coming at them, and unless they shifted at once . . .

The hoof was right out. They could move. Just as well, Robin thought afterwards, for if Ribbons had not been un-squelched, the wave would have enveloped her, drowned her, not just taken her with it as it did.

As it also took Robin.

Robin's first sensation was one of doing a complete cartwheel, then another, another, just as she had as a child, but where she had performed those on soft grass, she whirled now in muddy waters, over and over, desperately trying to get her head above water even for a brief moment to grab a breath and ease her choking lungs. It would be a freak flow, she knew, probably from some weakened storage tank that had collapsed from unusual pressure, it would be more than just the rain turning the small gutter into a banker. The result either would spread out on both sides to form a shallow lake, and she hoped for that, or, if there was any depression ahead, race further downwards to join and swell a lower level. If it did the latter, it would take her with it, so Robin determined not to let that happen, determined to grab the first impeding thing that offered.

She wondered sickeningly about Ribbons. The filly would be able to swim, of course, but never in a flood like this. She did not know whether her girl had been swirled away before or after her ... but she did know that if she didn't get her own head up soon and grab another breath she wouldn't be worried about anything any more. At that moment she did surface, and in the unnatural dark that had taken over she saw something brown, forlorn and submerged up to her darling nose, that nose Robin had stroked so often.

'Ribbons!' she called, and grabbed at the filly.

The two of them made a much more effective buffer against the stream than only one could have done. After some desperate but stubborn dual resistance, Robin felt they were gaining a little ground. Gaining ground literally, she knew presently. She felt her feet actually touching mud, and knew that if they stopped together they could make it to that bank she could now see through the rain-grey gloom, the bank of a tiny island that suddenly seemed to have sprung up. It would be some elevated section that had escaped the water's rush.

'Hold on, darling,' she told Ribbons, and Ribbons held.

Inch by inch, impeded every fraction of those inches by sticky mud, the flood still racing by them, the pair reached the tiny bank, edged up, and then, exhausted, stopped.

Ribbons lay down. She was breathing heavily, and, copying her, Robin lay down, too, and for some time they let the world and the flood pass by.

And the flood did. It must have been just as Robin had thought, a freak flow from some storage source. It could even be the Nooroo storage; their old tank, like everything else on the homestead, had been badly in need of repair or renewal.

'But never repair or renewal when it comes to you, my Ribbons,' Robin said proudly. 'Do you know, my girl, that you probably saved my life simply by being there?'

Ribbons looked back, saying the same to Robin with her soft eloquent eyes ... and it came as a shock to Robin when Tamar Warren's voice boomed: 'What in tarnation are you doing out there with my filly?'

He was standing on the bank of the little gutter that had turned into a river, but a river that was already diminishing, and he was glaring across at the small formed island at Robin and Ribbons.

Any relief that help was at hand that might have comforted Robin dropped away in the man's words. *My* filly, he had called. Somehow it never had occurred to her that along with the homestead, as well as the tractor, crops, poultry, pigs, sheep, the rest, had gone – Ribbons. Ribbons was hers, she had been present at her first shaky beginnings, she had knelt after her birth and wiped her lovingly, assured the bewildered small thing that everything was all right, that she was here, and safe, and belonging.

And now this man was saying: 'My filly', and Ribbons didn't belong. Across the lessening space of water, Robin glared back at him.

'Are you taking up residence there?' he called next, and

78

there was an irritated note in his voice.

'It's too deep to cross,' she answered sulkily.

'Yes, it would certainly reach your ankles,' he agreed with sarcasm.

She tested the water and found he was right. 'It was deep before,' she defended.

'Your – my – storage tank collapsed,' he explained. 'The flow is finished now. Had I known just how much disrepair I faced in Nooroo I might have had second thoughts.'

'I wish you *had* had them,' she cried back angrily. 'Have them now!'

'Can you buy me out, then?' As she did not answer he put out his hand and helped her over the last few yards to where he stood. She towed Ribbons behind her.

It was still raining, though a quiet rain now. But it was still wetting, and even though she was soaked already it was still unpleasant to be wet even more. When he said that they would make for the schoolhouse for a while, she did not object.

'Anyway,' he suggested thinly, 'I think it was where you were going.'

Again she did not reply.

There was not far to walk, and when they reached the little building she saw his car pulled up, so evidently it was no accident that he was here. He secured Ribbons, and while he unlocked the room with the key that she always concealed under an eave, and now instructed him, she gave the filly a quick rub.

'You need one yourself.' He stood at the opened door regarding her.

'I can wait.'

He shrugged. 'I wasn't offering,' he said.

She took as long as she could over Ribbons, then came inside. She was determined not to look at her desk, not with those sharp eyes on her, but it was no use, she could not help herself darting a quick anxious glance.

'It's all right.' His voice came coolly from the other side of the room. 'I have it here.'

'Have—'

'Have that thing that's worrying you. That trifle that brought you out on a day like this on my filly.' He held up the little weapon.

Relief at seeing the wretched object, knowing that it was not unaccounted for after all, pushed aside any curiosity as to how this man had become involved, any resentment because of the involvement, in a suddenly-gone-limp Robin. Sitting down on the nearest bench, she simply burst into tears.

'There,' he said, just as one would to a child. 'There.'

At any moment, Robin thought madly, he'll produce a handkerchief and direct: 'Blow.' But she didn't care. It was like coming out of a long dark tunnel, it was like sunshine after rain, the end of a nightmare. She blew on her own account and tidied her hair.

'How—' she began.

'How do I have possession of it?' he asked. 'I simply took it.'

'How did you know it was there?' she said next.

'Do you think I would have entrusted you with Mathew if I hadn't checked everything?'

'I didn't see you check.'

'I assure you I did.'

—Yes, she thought, he would do exactly that. She was unaware that she had tensed again. Mathew, she was thinking unreasonably, Tamar Warren would certainly consider him, consider everybody, but never consider—

'When I learned from Travers,' Warren went on, 'or was it Gillespie? I forget. However, when I found out the arrangement I was in full approval. You're isolated here and it's a crazy world these days. I was especially approving,' he added drily, 'when I learned that the thing wasn't loaded.'

'Wasn't—'

80

'Not *tellingly*,' he said. 'It was to give you something to hang on to *in case*, nothing else.'

'Well,' said Robin thinly, 'I'm glad I didn't know, then.' She was silent a while. 'Why, then, did you remove it? And when did you?'

'Because someone else could have had different ideas about loading,' he said, still drily, 'and I took it away before I left.'

'You had no right to.'

'I checked with the fathers and they agreed with me. You see, you were not the only one in the district less than happy about the Croker crowd.'

'Yet you employed their friend,' she shot at him.

'I didn't know,' he said shortly. 'I do know now. I also know to interview our next applicant personally.'

'There needn't be any.'

His brows raised on her. 'Taking on the housekeeping rôle yourself?'

'I won't be here, remember? Mathew will return to his mother, and Mathew was the only reason I was signed on.'

'His mother is coming out here,' Tamar Warren told Robin again. Then he added: 'And staying with you.'

'Staying with—' Although she knew Nooroo was now his she could not conceal her note of resentment at not being consulted first.

'Naturally,' he reminded her coolly, 'I can't have her at Glenville.'

'The all-male staff,' she nodded. 'Then why not put the new housekeeper there?'

'I would still require one at Nooroo,' he reminded her.

'But I'll be leaving,' she persisted.

'You seem in a great hurry all at once.'

'I'm not, but that was the arrangement.'

'I've altered it.'

'But I haven't agreed.'

'No, yet I think you will.' He was looking straight at her, and it was with difficulty, and that fact angered her, but it was still difficult, to withdraw her own glance.

'You're meaning because of Nooroo?' she said.

'What else?' A small smile.

'I have to go some time, haven't I?'

He neither replied nor commented, but she could feel that look of his continuing, even though she had succeeded at last in looking away herself.

'There's still no need for a housekeeper,' she said presently. Then, a little recklessly, suddenly feeling a desperate need to stop that penetrating look: 'Either I or Mathew's mother can cope.'

'Lilith has had a bad time,' he stated. 'I intend her to do nothing at all ... unless it's—' He did not finish, but there was a sudden gentle curve to his long firm lips.

Inexplicably irritated, Robin said baldly: 'You have plans for your stepmother, then?' For some unrecognized reason she emphasized that stepmother.

Tamar answered her quietly. He said: 'I can't imagine now I ever thought of her as that. She's far too young.' A pause. 'Far too lovely.'

'And once loved by your father.' Again Robin spoke deliberately.

'Yes.' He said it tightly as though the saying hurt him, which probably it did, and Robin bit her lip.

Presently she proffered: 'I didn't give you my sympathy, Mr. Warren. I do now.'

'There's no need. One hears often of release, but with Father it was that.' He was silent a painful moment. 'Shall we shut the place up now? The rain has stopped.'

'I expect,' Robin shrugged as they did so, 'it will be a case of really shutting up soon, or rather shutting down. The pupils are dimishing day by day.'

'The fleece is turning gold again,' he borrowed from Robin.

'Mathew is back at Nooroo,' he told her as they went

out. 'He was at a loose end when Noel went back again, so I promptly returned him. I can't abide unhappy kids. He's certainly taken to my manager. And that's another reason why I'd prefer Lilith over at Nooroo, he'd have both of them then.'

'Why did you drive out here?' Robin asked him.

'It was quite plain to me when you weren't at Nooroo, or Ribbons either, where you would head. And the same reason was why you were in that uncompromising position last night, wasn't it? You were about to spill out your cares to Noel and ask him what to do.'

His uncanny ability to read her, to size her up, angered Robin. 'Propriety. Convention. And now uncompromising! Are we still in the Victorian age?' she asked with sarcasm. 'Yet I was given to believe you had studied abroad – the U.K., the States.'

'Yet still a country boy at heart,' he baited.

'Apart from the words you use I'm still to see it. However' ... ungraciously ... 'thank you for making that rescue gesture.'

'You had the filly,' he reminded her.

'Your filly,' she said coldly.

'Of course.'

They closed the schoolroom door behind them. 'What about Ribbons?' Robin asked, looking at his car.

'We'll travel slowly and you can lean out and tow her. I think we should have to go slowly anyway, it might be all over, but there are still a lot of sticky spots.'

There were still several danger spots as well, they found, lower level paddocks where the tops of any scrub that had not been washed away now bobbed up and down like cabbage tops, but the water was quickly disappearing, and what was not running away was being thirstily absorbed into the porous ground.

'It wasn't good rain,' the man said, 'that would be a steady initial flow and a satisfactory follow-up. However, when you have smiling land like this, it takes more than a

83

flood to bring a frown.' His voice, Robin noted, was suddenly warm and sincere.

'You love it,' she said spontaneously.

'Did you doubt it?' He took his eyes off the road a moment to ask that of her.

'No, but—' She hesitated, suddenly warm herself because of the warmth he had just shown, shown for something she loved as well.

'Yes, Miss Mansfield?'

The formal address stiffened Robin. Admittedly she called him Mr. Warren, but for him to call her Miss Mansfield after he had called that Pat Pat, Ginny Ginny . . . and Mathew's mother Lilith—

'But what about Mrs. Warren?' she asked coldly. 'Is she of the same land mind?'

He was negotiating a difficult curve, the car slipping in the mud, Ribbons giving a whicker of distaste, but he found time to toss smoothly: 'We'll be finding out, no doubt.'

Then suddenly his blandness left him. Turning briefly to Robin, he said with urgency:

'I only hope she is.'

CHAPTER SIX

THOUGH it was a less than conclusive reply, Robin chose to find in it a definite conclusion. This man sitting beside her, she concluded, intended to marry the young widow.

For a son who apparently had been so attached to his father, it all rather shocked Robin. Yet, she thought, many might consider it a compliment to his father's good taste.

She did not care about it herself, though, and she felt her withdrawal even further away from the driver's seat. He must have sensed it, for he shot her a quick questioning look. She looked secretly back. He was near-handsome enough, affluent and eligible enough, she thought, to marry anyone, so why, why—

Inexplicably irritated at herself, inexplicable since what this man did or did not do was of no interest to her, Robin turned her glance to the soaked landscape.

'It wears off,' she said vaguely of the drenched terrain.

'I'm hoping it will.' His words, on the other hand, were not vague. It was apparent he was speaking of something else, and Robin sensed that it was Lilith Warren's ordeal over his father's death. Tamar obviously wanted that ghost laid so that he—

'When does she come?' Robin asked abruptly, and flushed as he raised politely inquiring brows on her though he must know to whom she referred.

'Mrs. Warren,' she said impatiently, impatient at his assumed lack of understanding.

'You could have been referring to the new housekeeper,' he said mildly.

'I was not.'

'Then Lilith will be here within two weeks.'

They were running up the peppercorn drive now, the berries that had been tossed down in the rain making a squelchy sound and turning the track into green and pink under their wheels. As they rounded the bend they saw Mathew having a fine time in a little lake in front of the homestead that the storm had left behind.

'It's a beaut,' he called enthusiastically, 'I've launched boats and made canals and now I'm doing a dam. Will this lake last long, Ragsy?'

'Ragsy?' The man picked it up and shot Robin a quick amused look.

'It's just a name we had,' she said, unamused.

'I'm glad you have restricted it to something between the two of you, it's hardly a complimentary tag.'

'It was just fun.'

'Yet it must have had a basis,' he puzzled. 'But of course' . . . enlightened . . . 'you're Robin. Ragged Robin. I saw one in England.' He was pulling up the car evidently by feel alone, for his eyes were on her, not the end of the drive.

'Mathew was Pablo,' Robin said a little desperately.

'You told!' accused Mathew, overhearing. 'You never answered me, will the lake last?'

'No.'

'Nothing should,' said the man, and Robin interpreted it that he meant grief for a very young, very lovely widow.

She turned stiffly to thank him, bid goodbye to him, but saw that he was getting out of the car as well. He walked behind her into the homestead. Why not? she thought resentfully as she often thought; it's his.

'I could do with a cuppa,' he said. 'Can you make tea?'

'Of course I can make tea.'

'Sorry, but I did notice that Ginny handled that side of

Nooroo.'

'Mrs. Mansfield,' said Robin deliberately, 'preferred being indoors.'

'Yes, Ginny would prefer domesticity,' he nodded casually, ignoring, or perhaps not hearing, Robin's formality.

'So,' he observed, returning again to Robin, 'you can cook, too.'

'And what does that "too" stand for?'

'Noel informs me that you're a dab hand to have around a station.'

'I try to be,' said Robin. 'I love it.'

'Don't overdo it, that's all. Two fillies and a young stallion are arriving tomorrow,' he went on. 'I told you I intended to supply my own needs. Before I look them over don't go getting any ideas about riding them.'

'Why not?'

He said the worst thing he could to Robin, he answered: 'They might not be amateur stuff.'

Amateur stuff! She stiffened. If Noel had not come in at that moment she would have said a few things to him. Instead she turned and went to the kitchen . . . to make a very indifferent pot of tea and to find only soggy biscuits to go with it.

'Well,' she defended as later Tamar looked distastefully at the unappetising offering, 'how was I to know it was going to rain and send them like that?'

'How, indeed! And how could you run up some scones instead if you didn't know how?'

'I do know.'

'As you know how to make tea.'

Noel came in with a pacific: 'She's a first-class jill on a station.'

Tamar Warren said warningly, a warning to Robin: 'We've spoken about that.'

Indeed you have, thought Robin, but for all her resentment she did not say anything aloud. There was something about Mr. Tamar Warren that—

Over the break the men spoke about the cotton Warren intended trying; cotton was doing well in the northwest.

'By the present look of things,' mused Noel, 'you would say that rice would do better, but tomorrow all that moisture will have disappeared.'

Robin let them talk without adding any words of her own, which was unthought-of for her; the land was her very life blood and she could never keep out of such conversation. But she did today. When she could, she excused herself and went out to find Mathew. He had emptied his lake by means of a long canal into the pig pen and was as muddy as a little pig himself.

'Your mother wouldn't know you,' Robin said. 'Did you know she'll be right here at Nooroo in two weeks?'

'Yes, all of us together,' approved Mathew. 'It will be a proper family – a man, a lady, and a child. Me.' He added generously, 'And you, Ragsy.'

'You think that makes a family?' asked Robin. 'I mean the man and the lady part?'

'Of course. A father, a mother, then me.' Again, generously: 'And you.'

'But Noel isn't your father.'

'Pretend, of course.'

'What will I be?'

'My sister?' Mathew asked.

'That's very nice of you, Pablo. Now you have a sister and a brother.' – How long would it be just a brother? she wondered.

'I haven't any brother.'

'Mr. Warren, darling.'

'That was a stepbrother. Did you know about steps? They're not steps like steps ... oh, bother, the lake must be drying up.' Mathew looked with disappointment at the

88

canal that would certainly not reach the jig pen after all.

'Bath for you,' decreed Robin, and taking his hand she impelled him, half protesting, half laughing, up to the house.

Tamar was just leaving. He glanced at the boy, then at her, noticing their flushed and happy faces. 'So many facets,' he observed.

'What, Mr. Warren – I mean Tamar?' She corrected that quickly. Thank heavens, she thought, she would not need to much longer.

'Just when I rule out any domestic side to you I find a maternal side, yet the two usually go together.'

'One doesn't have to be a cook to be a parent,' she pointed out.

'Yet they still usually coincide. The child has to be fed and the mother likes to prepare the food.' He yawned slightly as he said it as though the subject fairly bored him. 'Don't forget what I told you,' he tossed as he went down to the car.

'What did he tell?' asked Mathew.

Robin generally had enough sense to keep her own counsel, had the caution not to confide things to do with adults to children, but she was in a childish mood herself today, and that 'amateur stuff' that Tamar Warren had tossed at her had gone deep.

'He told me not to ride the new horses when they come.'

'Are there going to be new horses?' thrilled Mathew.

'Yes. Two girls and a boy. And later on there'll be foals. If you were here you would like that.'

Mathew looked at Robin with surprise. 'I'll be here with my mother.'

'It takes a while for foals, Pablo, the same as it does with babies.'

'But I'll be here,' repeated Mathew. He seemed so certain that Robin wondered if Tamar had said something to him today. Had he prepared the boy for a different relationship than stepbrother? Yet Mathew had corrected her with stepbrother instead of brother, said that steps were not like ordinary steps.

'What makes you think you'll be here? Your mother is only coming to fetch you,' she reminded him.

'She'll stay and we'll be a family,' Mathew persisted confidently. He clamoured for more information about the horses.

'They'll be young,' said Robin.

'How young?'

'Oh, a year or so.'

'That's very young,' frowned Mathew.

'You multiply it for horses when you compare it with yourself,' explained Robin. 'It makes it a lot more.'

Mathew said admiringly . . . and no doubt with a view to postponing his bath for as long as possible: 'You know everything in the world about horses, don't you, Ragsy.'

'Not at all.'

'And,' continued Mathew, 'if I were you I'd ride his horses.'

'We all have to do what we're told,' Robin contributed, regretting now that she had confided what she had. She added: 'And I'm telling you to get in the bath.'

'I will,' agreed Mathew, 'because I 'spect I need it.' He regarded a muddy knee with interest. 'But you don't have to, Ragsy, because you don't need, do you?'

'Need a bath?' she interpreted deliberately.

'No,' he said, 'I mean you needn't not ride. Because you're the bestest rider, so he shouldn't tell you that.'

It was gratifying to be praised, but Robin had recovered from her pique. 'If you're not in that bath in one minute . . .'

Mathew ran down the passage.

When Noel had praised Robin to Tamar as being a

first-class hand he had spoken the truth. Especially, Robin knew he could have added, in the understanding of horses. Robin could not remember when Grandfather had first taken her out to the boundary with him, but it had been his boast that he had had to carry her to the saddle because she still couldn't walk. That was exaggeration, of course, but Robin could not recall not being perfectly at home on the back of a horse.

From that expertise had sprung other specialities. Like not waiting to unfasten a gate when you could fly over it. Like changing paddocks for a flock of sheep that looked far too large for one girl and one dog to handle.

Being inexperienced with cattle, particularly of the Brahma that Glenville was favouring, Robin was currently listening to everything that Noel told her. He was pleased with her progress, she knew, and that was why he had told Tamar she was a dab hand. When a message came the next morning from Glenville to move a Brahma mob from behind the hill and Noel was away, she had no hesitation in tackling the job herself. She had done a little already with Noel, and considered herself perfectly capable.

Ribbons had recovered completely from her wet adventure, and obviously enjoyed her run over paddocks that did not feel dust-dry under her hooves as they usually did. The softer going suited her, and when Robin guided her towards a gate she took it perfectly.

'Ragsy!' cried a distant little voice, 'wait for me, you know I can't do that yet.'

Robin wheeled round and saw that Pablo was behind her on his small mount. He rode quite well, but he certainly couldn't jump, as he had complained. She cantered back to the gate, but did not open it.

'You can't come, Mathew, this is for big people only.'

'I'm good. You said so.'

'Sheep-good, not cattle. Not yet. And that's what I'm on now – the Brahma.'

'How can I be good if I don't learn?' protested Mathew.

'You'll learn, but not today. Now back you go' She waited till he turned round, then spurred Ribbons on again.

It was not a large assignment requiring the help of Wattie, perhaps several of the Glenville men, otherwise Robin would not have tackled it alone. She was proud of her ability, but she was not a fool. She came up on the small mob and reckoned they would be no trouble at all.

She roused them and got them on the go. Behind the hill should not take more than an hour.

They were quite eager to move; like everything and everybody the world over, the distant pasture was the desired one. Robin smiled her satisfaction as they trotted in orderly rhythm round the base of the slope.

She did not know what changed the pattern; she had learned from Noel that it took only one beast to break up a course, the same as with sheep, but cattle were different from sheep, less capricious, especially a small manageable, one could almost say domestic, mob like this.

But Robin was to learn that basically, once disturbed, whether small or large, mobs were all the same. Suddenly one of the beasts changed his mind about direction, and at once the small crowd of them was changing course. Digging her heels into Ribbons to hurry her forward, Robin wondered what had disturbed the initial beast, then she saw out of the corner of her eye that it was Mathew. The little boy must have returned, or perhaps he had never left at all, then he had made some small movement – the slightest movement of all, Noel had told her, could divert a beast. Now, and she saw it with horror, the boy was standing on a tiny rise right in the path of the new direction.

'Mathew!' The voice cut above the heavy clop of the hooves, a strong resonant voice, a very male voice.

'Mathew, clap your hands, clap hard!'

There was dominance in the order, a command that could not be ignored, even by a child dumbly fascinated by an approaching horned army. The little boy clapped, and the beasts deviated slightly. Robin took the opportunity of the small deviation to ride beside them and edge them inwards again. A man came up and rode beside her. Between them, in minutes, the mob was orderly again.

But not Tamar Warren. He was thunderingly angry. With a brush of his arm . . . a whip at the end of it . . . he took over from Robin. One look at his face decided her not to offer her services any more. She pulled Ribbons up and cantered across to Mathew.

'Why are you here, Pablo?' she demanded.

'I just wanted to learn, Ragsy,' he appealed.

'A nice time you chose, then! What did you do to panic the beasts?'

'Nothing.'

Well, that could be right, Robin sighed; Noel had told her it often took only the brush of an eyelash to start a rush.

'You shouldn't have come,' she said weakly, and left it at that. Probably the boy would be in trouble, anyway, from Tamar.

But it was Robin who was in trouble. Galloping back from the other side of the hill, the man prompted Mathew smartly up on his little mount, then hissed: 'Home', accompanying it with a smack on the pony's rump.

'That should be administered elsewhere,' he said as the child cantered off.

'I don't think he intended any harm.'

'I don't think so, either, if I did I wouldn't have slapped the pony. However, it wasn't the youngster I was referring to, it was you whom I wanted to feel the weight of my hand.' He glowered down on her.

'I can believe that!' Robin glowered back.

'Then come forward with some explanation, or you will be feeling it.'

Robin started to retort that it would be the last slapping he would be inflicting, then thought better of it.

'I'm sorry about Mathew,' she submitted, 'but I did send him home.'

'Rather an unrealistic thing to do,' he commented brusquely, glancing significantly around him, at all the fascination this must offer to a little boy.

'Yes, it was, but I didn't know he'd followed me until I was nearly here, and I was so anxious to do the job I wouldn't take the time off to see he went back as I said.'

She spoke honestly but hopelessly; she did not think for a moment he would accept such an inadequate story, even though it was the truth. But the obvious truth must have decided him not to pursue the whys and wherefores of the episode.

'I suppose on the other hand,' he said, 'I should be pleased at your enthusiasm, even if it was premature.'

'Premature?' she queried,

'You're not up to the cattle yet, Miss Mansfield. After all, as well as being with sheep all your life and all the lives that preceded you, you're female.'

'Does it make a difference?'

'A steer is harder handling than a ball of wool. When I phoned that instruction it was for Noel, not his jilleroo. When I want you to do a job, I'll stipulate it.'

'Yes, sir,' she said.

He looked sharply at her for any evidence of impudence, found nothing, then unexpectedly brought Ribbons across and gave her a hand to mount the filly. He got on his own mount and rode back to Nooroo beside her.

On the way he gave her a lot of hints on cattle, not the orthodox ones that Noel had primed her in, but little seemingly inconsequential things that she suspected would probably have a lot of consequence.

Like taking it easy, because the beasts sensed relaxation, so relaxed, too. Like not rushing in if a rush started, because that could be fatal. Like keeping an eye on the stagey fellows because they were the ones who generally started trouble. Like letting a fellow go if you were by yourself, or unable to rope, as she was undoubtedly unable.

'Could I be taught?' Robin said demurely.

'I'll try you out before I answer that.' He handed her a length of rope and rode away from her.

Robin could barely suppress her giggles. This was something she could do; Grandfather Mansfield had been more proud of her skill in this than he had been over any school report. She had seen him do it once, then had clamoured: 'Me, too!' She had been an apt pupil. With a twist and a weave now she roped the man easily, then, sitting back in the saddle, watched for his reaction.

'All right,' he awarded sparsely, 'you've proved a point, but don't forget I'm not a moving target. Now finish the job.'

'How do you mean?'

'You bring me in, naturally.'

As she still looked at him, he snapped: 'You wouldn't leave the thing there with a rope around it.'

'No,' she agreed, 'but—'

'Finish the job,' he called.

Slowly she collected the rope to her again, collected the man. Only, several yards from her, she found she could not finish it after all. Dropping the rope on his saddle, she turned Ribbons sharply in the opposite direction. As she galloped off she heard his low laugh.

But there was no laughter a few days afterwards.

The nucleus of Glenville's future horses arrived in padded boxes, and, since the larger estate was being reallocated for better usage, the two fillies and the young stallion were delivered to Nooroo.

Mathew was enchanted, and indeed the soft dappled grey and the bright chestnut girls would have won a heart not overly inclined to horseflesh. The stallion was rather a different proposition, he was a very big bay, extremely handsome, and with obviously large ideas about himself, or so Robin judged by the proud holding of the head, the impatient, almost supercilious play of the fine hooves when not in action as though inactivity frankly bored him.

'Not quite my idea of the perfect domestic sire,' judged Noel by Robin's side. 'Possibly not Tamar's, either, for the fellow was catalogue bought.' He scrutinized the fillies. 'They appear suitable enough, though I understand Tamar chose them personally himself.'

Tamar came over that evening to look over his purchases. Robin was not there, but Noel reported later that he had been pleased about the fillies but had put the stallion aside for a different purpose from the one for which he had been purchased.

'Probably he'll be put to service eventually,' Noel said, 'but only after he's exercised some of that obvious excess self-satisfaction away. Immediately Tamar wants a more settled type for the fillies. He thinks he'll be able to fit the bill locally. Ferrys have a young upstanding fellow.'

'Nightcap,' nodded Robin. 'A darling, and very amenable.' She asked Noel what was planned meanwhile for the bay.

'I suppose Tamar will take him over to Glenville in time. He's a horse who'll need a strong hand.'

Robin could have accepted that, but what she could not accept was a man's hand. And that was what Tamar Warren said to her at his next inspection of the three additions, Robin present this time.

'The fillies are amiable,' he said, 'but don't get ideas about the stallion. My previous warning still stands. That fellow needs a man's hand.'

A man's hand. Men.

'It makes me sick,' Robin said.

'Me, too,' agreed Mathew, looking with dislike at the rice on his plate (for Robin had spoken her thoughts at lunch) since, pending the housekeeper's arrival at Nooroo, Robin, who was cook, was saving time by boiling up large quantities of Mathew's despised rice and hoping for the best, though not often achieving it, by adding different adornments.

'I know you're not keen, Pablo,' Robin said of the rice, 'but I'm very busy, and Cooky will come tomorrow.'

And the next day it was because of the new housekeeper that the thing occurred.

Ribbons was being shod at Glenville. Noel had the car, and the jeep still was out of repair while waiting for an engine part, replacements in Yarani having to come a long way.

Besides the jeep, the telephone was not functioning. It had been making curious noises all the morning, and Mathew reported that every time he answered a ring there was nobody saying anything but there was a lot of crackly stuff.

'Mumbo-jumbo,' nodded Robin.

'Is that a foreign language?'

'Kind of. Oh, well, if anyone wants us, it's just too bad.'

But it was the new cook who found it just too bad. She arrived in the hire car from town, a plump pleasant woman who looked, Mathew whispered by Robin's side, like someone who would make lots of apple pies.

'Yes, she does look like that,' agreed Robin, pleased with what she saw. So very different from Pat, she appreciated. She smiled at the woman and the woman beamed back, a beam that changed to consternation some minutes later, the taxi departed now ... *and with one of her bags.*

'The one with my photographs in,' cried Mrs. Mac-Pherson. 'Anything but that!'

Robin sympathized with her. Probably she was a widow, by her apparent age a widow whose children had married, then before their mother had left for the country had given her copious photos of her grandchildren. Without doubt, Robin thought, she was one of those motherly souls who would put a big value on family photos.

'We'll recover it, of course,' said Robin, knowing it would be cold comfort for Mrs. MacPherson, who was obviously a woman who had to surround herself with her loved ones at once.

She went uselessly to the phone, anticipating that it would still be out of order. It had not functioned well since the rain. Once again it crackled.

'Mumbo-jumbo?' asked Mathew.

'Yes.'

'I know you think I'm making a fuss,' apologized Mrs. MacPherson, 'but—' The tears came to her eyes and she turned away.

'It will be all right,' reaffirmed Robin.

'Oh, I know no one would want little Sandra's picture, or young Peter, or the twins, or—'

Crackle, went the receiver, and Robin put it down.

There was no car to drive. There was no way to ring. If she could get across to another farm she could ring from there. But there was no Ribbons to take her.

But there were three horses.

When Robin went to the stables she had no ideas of disobeying Tamar, in spite of Mathew's advice, she had full intention of riding one of the fillies. But, at the door of the stables, she recalled that already the young stallion had been taken away from the fillies, that the girls had been transferred to the far northern paddock by Wattie. Also that it had taken him nearly all the morning to do it, since it was several miles away.

She bit her lip, all the time eyeing the big bay. He seemed a different identity today, more amiable, which was not surprising; no horse could be really amicable after a long stretch in a box.

He looked back at Robin hopefully, and she knew he was anxious for a run, poor dear. He had good legs, she noted, it must be agony not to let himself go.

She approached him, but before she reached him he came up to her. When she touched him, he stood very quiet.

'I shouldn't, you know,' she said confidentially to the horse, 'I was ordered not to.'

She had a tantalizing vision of galloping across to Glenville, Tamar sitting smoking on the verandah and getting up incredulously from his chair as she hurdled over the final fence to come to a smooth halt on the drive, the big bay docilely waiting for her to dismount, Tamar Warren struck dumb in admiration of her skill.

Only, even though the thought enticed, she would not do that, she would go to Glennifers, only several miles further in the opposite direction, and ring for Mrs. MacPherson's bag from there.

Mathew had not followed her to the stables, which saved her the trouble of concocting a reason for taking out the bay . . . which he wouldn't believe, anyway, he would claim she had listened to what he had urged. But looking up to the house she saw he was still indoors, probably pumping the housekeeper about her grandchildren.

Noel was out. Wattie was at work with the pigs. There was no one to watch.

She saddled the bay, who stood as docile as she could wish, then walked him out.

He was a tall horse to mount, but to Robin that was no trouble. A moment later they were flying across the first field. The stallion was behaving beautifully, he had a long springy stride and was comfortable to ride. Everything was going well . . . except, and a big except, they were going in the wrong direction. They were going to Glenville, not Glennifers. Robin pulled the horse gently at first, then, when he did not obey, more definitely. When he took no notice, *very definitely* . . . and that was the last thing she clearly remembered.

She stayed on . . . she could not have said how, it must have been by instinct, from years of staying on, whatever happened, but that was all she was aware of, that she was still on.

On, as they took fences, on, as they crossed the creek, not losing a pace, on over the flat beside the Glenville eastern ridge. On, past a herd of white horns. On, past a thicket of gums with rough roots ready to trip an unfamiliar horse.

In her vision, Robin had seen herself coming up to the Glenville homestead, only it had been just a dream, never really intended. Now, as in the dream, she was actually approaching the home, that home she had never seen in spite of the fact it was as near as next door, a house wavering so much that she wasn't really seeing it, nor seeing its wavering squire . . . Tamar Warren . . . who, just as in her vision, was rising from a chair on the verandah to watch her come.

Her vision had stopped at that, had stopped at the bay's halt as she dismounted, she had not got up to Tamar Warren's reaction. And reception. The reaction she did not see properly, she was still wavering. But the reception she felt, if she did not see.

Calling sharply to a groom to take the bay, so sharply that the boy actually raced across, Tamar took hold of her.

He took her inside. Took her to a room that must be an office, she thought vaguely, from its desk and its account books.

Then he was shaking her. Shaking her so that everything wavered even more for her. He was looking down with eyes so angry that they glittered. He was saying in a barely controlled voice: 'I told you, remember? I told you a man's hands only. By God, Robin, I'd like these hands on you right now!'

CHAPTER SEVEN

For a moment Robin thought she really was going to feel that large cattleman hand, and involuntarily she stepped back. Her movement did something to Tamar Warren. The muscle stopped jerking by the side of his tightened mouth, the vein stopped throbbing in his temple.

'Stop flinching,' he said contemptuously, and the two words were enough to send Robin's chin tilting proudly again.

'I'm sorry for disobeying,' she said in an un-sorry voice. 'I know what you ordered, even though Pablo—' She stopped herself in time, but not time enough to prevent the angry focus again of those glittering eyes.

'Yes?' Tamar Warren asked. 'Even though Mathew what, Miss Mansfield?'

'Nothing.'

'Even though what?' he persisted, and he stepped forward a pace, bringing their proximity to the same distance as they had been before she had withdrawn. — Flinched had been Tamar Warren's word.

'Mathew believes in my horsemanship,' she tried to evade.

'You really mean,' he deciphered, 'he urged you to go ahead and take no notice of what I said. I'll have a word with that young fellow!'

'Why should you?' she called furiously, furious for the little boy.

'Why should I take a stand on connivance?' he questioned her.

'Why should you speak to him at all? You're not his parent.' Almost she added, 'Yet.'

'Quite right,' he agreed. 'The boy has no fatherly control at the moment.'

'No, not at the moment,' Robin agreed shortly. Presently she said in a more reasonable tone: 'Don't take it out on Pab— on Mat, please. It was only something said in passing. I'd told him he needed a bath, then he very kindly said I didn't need—'

'A riding lesson?'

'Well, something like that.'

'He was wrong, wasn't he?'

'No.'

'Think again, Miss Mansfield.'

'I rode the bay efficiently enough.'

'Even took some fences and a creek in an admirable manner. But—' He stood, eyes narrowed now, half smiling down at her, an amused but demeaning semi-curve of his lips.

She waited for him to finish the smile, because there was something more to be said yet, from the shape of that mouth.

'But did you intend to come to *Glenville*?' he asked.

'Of course I did. I mean ... That is ...' Her voice trailed off. 'How' ... wretchedly ... 'how would you know?' How *did* this man know? she suffered. How did he always know?

'I know you wouldn't come here of your own free will, you never have. The curiosity of woman is often acclaimed, but I will say that for you, you're not curious ... as far as I'm concerned. No, Miss Mansfield, I believe the horse dominated you and took you where *he* wanted. So, in spite of the fences, the creek, the ability to stay on, you do need a lesson, don't you? The lesson of control.'

She did not reply.

He sat down at his desk and waved her to a seat opposite. After a moment she complied.

'Why did you do it?' he asked. 'You don't look a fool to me, Noel's reports on you are anything but the reports on a dimwit, but still you took out that obviously difficult young stallion.'

'He was a lamb,' Robin insisted.

'Because he got his own way. If you'd gone against him—'

'I did.'

'Gone against him more strongly there might be a different story to tell.' He ignored her interruption. 'You mightn't be upright as you are now. I mean that, Miss Mansfield. He's a difficult fellow and will need a lot of concentration on him.'

'Male concentration?'

'Certainly.'

'Yours!' she snapped.

'Of course.'

Frustrated, she said, borrowing from Noel: 'He wasn't a good choice for a sire.'

'No, but he was catalogue bought. I went on measurements alone – measurements, as I expect you know, are advisable in breeding. Had I seen the boy—'

'You wouldn't have bought him?'

'No, I think I would have. He has spirit, I like spirit.'

Yes, thought Robin, you've admired Lilith's spirit many times.

'However,' Tamar was saying, 'I will not use him in the stud yet.' He was thoughtful for a while, probably on the subject of the stud, but any ideas that she was out of the discussion were cut short by his abrupt: 'You haven't answered me yet. Why did you take the horse out?'

'The phone wasn't working. Noel had the car, the jeep still isn't going. Ribbons is over here being shod. The fillies were in the far northern paddock and would have taken me the best part of an hour to catch and saddle. There was nothing else to do.'

'So you had an urgent message?'

'Cooky had one. Mrs. MacPherson arrived in the hire car today, and the taxi went off with one of her cases. It was the precious one with the family photos, she was really unhappy.'

'And you went along with that?'

'Yes, I did.' Again Robin tilted her chin, this time in defence of Mrs. MacPherson whom she supported in this, no matter what that monster opposite thought.

'Good,' he said unexpectedly. 'So would I. What did you intend to do about it?'

'Ring the hire car firm.'

'From where? And don't say here,' he warned, 'because you weren't bound for here.'

'You're very clever,' she admired sarcastically. 'How did you find out?'

'Because Mathew rang up from Nooroo and told me.'

'The phone is out of order,' she stated again, privately reminding herself never to underrate the apparent inattention of little boys again.

'Evidently he was testing it for mumbo-jumbo, or so he said, and the wires must have righted themselves. He told me he'd seen you on the bay headed in this direction, and that it would be about Mrs. MacPherson's bag. Then he said not to be angry, because you really were the bestest rider in the world, and he himself had advised you to ride the horse.'

'Pab— Matthew talks too much.'

'For his own good,' agreed Tamar. 'No,' as Robin raised an anxious face, 'I'm not going to whack him, though if he had been at hand at the moment it might be a different story – telling you to take no notice of me indeed!'

'It was more my fault,' he corrected. 'Incidentally, where were you bound?'

'Glennifers. Some miles further, but—'

'Safer?'

She bit her lip and kept quiet.

'The bag,' he broke him, 'has been traced and will come out by special delivery at once. Tonight Mrs. MacPherson will sleep surrounded by her loved ones.'

'Then all is well,' Robin murmured.

'No cheers for you,' he reminded her. He got up. 'Now you're here you may as well look round the house you've always avoided.'

'I've never been interested.'

'Don't you ever stop lying?' he asked.

'I haven't been interested and I'm not interested now. Anyway, why should I look? I won't even be seeing much more of Nooroo, let alone the boss's palace.'

'It's not a palace, it's a comfortable home that I would like to make more comfortable, or perhaps more attractive, still.' He paused. 'For a certain reason.'

Robin knew the reason and she felt like inserting: 'Then wait till Lilith arrives and let her choose for herself.'

She began again: 'I'm not not interested—' but she did not quite finish.

Suddenly angry once more, he crossed to her and jerked her from where she sat. 'You'll damn well look,' he said, 'or else—'

'Or else?' Robin asked recklessly.

'Or I'll do what I intended to do when you came thundering up to the verandah.'

'A man's hand,' she taunted, not stepping back this time.

'The full weight of it,' he promised, but not stepping forward. However the warning was still there, and it was Robin who first evaded her gaze from his glittering eyes.

'Come on,' he pronounced, and led the way from the study.

Tamar had been right when he had guessed a long interest in Robin about Glenville. As a child she had gazed at it much more than she would have liked to admit. In spite of herself, of the way she had wanted to consider it, it had always been something of a castle — well, a castle, anyway, compared to Nooroo, compared to any of the Yarani homesteads. She supposed the two storeys had comprised the fascination; whereas every other house was a typical one-level Australian country home, the sort that sprawled not climbed, Glenville had climbed. Then the imposing drive, pines instead of peppercorns, the shrubbery, the gardens . . .

'I've no doubt,' Tamar Warren was drawling as he led Robin down a long gracious hall, 'you had splinters in your nose countless times as you peeped through the fence.'

'It would be a long peep,' Robin retorted, 'all those miles away.'

'Don't tell me you kept that distance,' he scorned.

'I did.'

'Lying again!'

'I am not.'

'Lying,' he insisted. 'You see, Miss Mansfield, I even watched you watching me one day, it would be . . . yes, some fifteen years ago.'

'It's you who are lying. I never even knew you existed.' She spoke hotly, for now she was speaking the truth. Well, semi-truth. She had known of him but never known him . . . even if she had, as he had just said, peeped.

'I saw you,' he repeated, enjoying her discomfort, 'knee-high to a grasshopper, front teeth missing. Oh, most certainly you were aware of this house.'

'Oh, yes, I knew there was a house,' bitterly.

'No call for resentment about mere bricks and mortar, surely?'

'No,' she agreed, 'only for the land, *our* land, that surrounded the bricks and mortar.'

He stopped abruptly, stopping her with him there in the hall. 'A part by the creek only, never house-embracing.' As she went to argue he held up his hand. 'Not now, please, I want you to criticize, to suggest. This house has had only males for many years, my mother died when I was a baby. I want to know how a woman sees it.'

'I'm not domesticated, remember?'

'Oh, yes, the scones, lack of,' he laughed. 'But still you might have a few ideas.'

'I think you should wait for Mathew's mother.'

'Perhaps. I know her taste is impeccable. But I would like you to see it, even if you can't suggest, and good heavens, woman, why can't you? You're female, after all, aren't you? Don't you ever want to belong to a house and not a horse?'

'I'm not that type,' Robin mumbled, 'I'm the outdoor sort.'

'You did think you might marry one day, though, didn't you?'

'No, I never did any thinking like that.'

'Lies and more lies. All women think in that marrying strain.'

'Well, if I did it was essentially a country marriage, one where my man needed me more beside him in a field than my waiting for him to come home to carve up the roast.'

'I note,' Tamar said, 'you stipulate country marriage. I think by that you mean a country fellow.'

'I didn't particularly mean it, it was just something to say.'

'But presumably if you envisaged yourself beside him in a field it would be a country background and a country bloke.'

'I just said it,' she persisted, 'to tell you I will be useless advising you about anything.'

'Unless it's a sick cow?' he suggested.

'So long as it's not curtains and floor covers and—'

'Running up scones,' he nodded. Then, humorously, 'Can you tell me why people run up scones and cakes?'

'I can't.'

'Well, you certainly don't. Run them up, I mean. But never mind, you're a good jilleroo, Noel reports, and the other can come later.' Before she could interject, he asked: 'How do you find this room?'

How did she find it? She found it perfectly beautiful. A little old and worn, but lovingly so. Good old things, she thought a little sadly, only grow more precious with age.

She was silent standing in the gold and russet parlour ... you had to call it parlour, for lounge, or even sitting-room, would never have done. Nooroo had never been beautiful. Her mother had hated the country, so disliked the house, and the father Robin could not remember had only lived on counting the days when they would be out of it. Her mother had made no attempt to improve it. Ginny had made no attempt, either, she had not even unpacked her bags. Ginny's city flat had been charming, but Nooroo had been left as Ginny found it, and that had been uninspired, functional, clumsy. This place now, apart from visits to school friends' places when she had been at boarding school, was Robin's first experience of a lovely home.

She followed him from room to room, not silent now from resentment, but quiet because she could find no words, because the house moved her so much.

The century, she thought, could have been the nineteenth, and actually that was what it would have been when Tamar Warren's grandfather had built it. The mahogany in it was that century, the grandfather clock the same time.

The kitchen had been modernized but could do with more renovation again. She murmured this, and he nodded. He took her to a library, not the functional study in which apparently he did his book work, but a formal library. It was as beautiful as the parlour ... though something seemed wrong.

'I think it's the curtains,' Robin murmured aloud. 'That long damask is depressing. Short white muslin, perhaps.'

'You amaze me,' he said sincerely. 'For a girl who only

comes alive on the back of a horse you're doing pretty well.'

She flushed, but could not help feeling pleased with herself. She followed him into another room . . . and there she stood.

It was a nursery, and quite obviously nothing had been done to it for many years.

'No children,' Tamar pointed out. 'I was the last, and even before me there was only one, my mother. Rather an unproductive lot, the Glenvilles, for which, no doubt, you would be well pleased.'

She did not reply, she could not have told him how the room touched her. An old slipper bath. A child's cradle. A picture or two, old-fashioned now, but charming and sweet. Everything small and delicate and loved.

'It's beautiful.' Her voice came a little choked, and she hoped he put it down to something in her throat.

'I've always thought so,' he said. 'I wanted a brother . . . a sister would have done. But it wasn't to be. Still' . . . he had moved to the window and pulled aside an old buttercup curtain . . . 'I feel it might be soon. – Ever get such ideas?'

'I don't go round looking at nurseries,' she said coldly. This was to be Lilith's house . . . Lilith's nursery.

'I'm sorry,' he said blandly, 'I should have known it was not your department. I hear cups. We'll go down and have tea. Then I'll drive you back.'

'Ribbons is here.'

'We'll go slowly as we did after the flood, and you can tow your girl.'

'There's no need.'

'There is need, you've done all the riding you're doing for today, Miss Mansfield. Now show me, please, if at least you can pour.' They had descended the stairs, and he pulled out a chair and nodded to a big pot that had been put on the table.

Feeling clumsy, inefficient, inadequate, un-female,

Robin complied ... doing what she knew she would do, with those eyes on her, spilling drops on the clean cloth.

'It's a bad spout,' excused Tamar formally, but there was a laugh there besides a polite excuse, a laugh at her.

Flushing, she handed him a plate of biscuits – crisp ones, not like her soggy offering. She saw the fresh laughter hanging in his eyes. All at once she was laughing herself.

'Good marks, Robin,' he awarded, and it was as unexpected as his unexpected use of her name. 'You can take it, girl.' Then abruptly the laughter was leaving him and he was just looking at her. Robin was just looking back.

It was an effort to take her glance away.

Robin was relieved to find, after Tamar had deposited her and Ribbons at Nooroo and left again without coming in, that Pablo was occupied with a new friend, Mrs. MacPherson. Robin had no wish to be questioned by the little boy over the riding incident. He knew she had been forbidden to mount the bay, and the fact that she had disobeyed, even though it had been his advice she do so, might have shocked him. As it should shock him, Robin sincerely believed. Even in this liberated age, children should have a respect for a grown-up's orders.

She found him in the kitchen with Cooky, a happy Cooky now because her bag had come back.

'All the children's photos are there,' announced Mathew. 'Sandra ... she's nine, Terence ... he's eight ... the twins, the new baby and—'

'And their mothers, my two dear daughters, but not, I must confess, the fathers,' Mrs. MacPherson smiled at Robin. She explained: 'I couldn't spare any more space, though they're good sons-in-law. I'm sure, dear, you consider this all a storm in a teacup.'

'We had a storm,' came in Mathew, 'but it was out-side.'

'I don't think that at all,' Robin assured Cooky, 'and I'm glad you have your family around you.'

'Sandra, Terence, Peter and Paul, Belinda Jane—' tabulated Mathew.

'I tell you what,' suggested Mrs. MacPherson, 'you just take Miss Robin and show her.'

'Can I?' Mathew bounced off.

The two women exchanged more smiles, then Robin followed the little boy down the passage.

How different a house, she could not help thinking as she went, from Glenville. Always Robin had had a sneaking feeling that Nooroo wasn't what it should be, she had thought it vaguely as a child, more definitely, if un-admittedly, as a schoolgirl, but occupied entirely with the outside of the homestead, any dismay she might have felt at the inside had been brief, there had been more pressing matters, like crops, like sheep to be moved, like pigs to be tended, so that general shabbiness, general don't care-ness, hadn't mattered so much.

Now, somehow, it did matter. For the first time Robin really felt ashamed. What sort of woman was she? What sort of woman did she seem to others? To – Tamar Warren?

But when she reached Mrs. MacPherson's room she was not ashamed. In the space of a few hours the house-keeper had made a little haven of it.

Flowers. (why didn't I think of that? vexed Robin.) Books. Pictures. Knick-knacks. Most of all the family photos. Her two daughters as babies, as schoolgirls, as brides. Their children as babies and schoolchildren. Mathew was excited as he brought each one up to Robin. He was probably missing the other pupils whose company he had enjoyed, though briefly, at school. What had Tamar said that day he had enrolled him? It had been companion-hungry. Well, it appeared he would become that again until his mother took him back to England, for it seemed an agreed fact that the little school would not re-open. Prosperity had not actually arrived for the sheep farmers, but certainly the future seemed brighter. The old affluent days might never be repeated, thought Robin, nor the days when wool was king, when the fleece was gold (though she had acclaimed that fleece bit herself many times) but with a greater variety of offerings in the productive basket, as most of the farmers were doing now, there seemed no need to go back to the last leaner years again.

'Cattle, cotton, crops, sunflowers,' she said aloud, and Mathew looked questioningly at her.

'Once it was nothing but sheep,' she told him. 'Now there's a mixed plate.'

'Where's the plate?' asked Mathew, looking as confused as he had been over Mrs. MacPherson's storm in a teacup.

'Just adults' silly talk, darling.'

'Yes,' Mathew heartily agreed.

But he approved of Mrs. MacPherson. He said: 'When I look at her I think of jellies and cakes and jam.'

'You really mean you don't think of rice,' interpreted Robin.

'Do you like her room, Ragsy?' he asked.

'Yes, Pablo, and it's given me an idea. We must do up your mother's room.'

'She hasn't as many photos as Mrs. MacPherson, only my really father, then that next one who was going to be, and of course, me.'

'We can still make it nice,' Robin said, thinking that that husband list seemed quite enough for the present.

She told Noel that night, a Noel frankly enjoying Mrs. MacPherson's offerings after Robin's. – 'Sorry, old girl,' he grinned when Mrs. MacPherson, accompanied by an eager Mathew, went out to bring in the next course, 'but you can be Jack of all trades but specialist in only one, and you're the finest hand a man ever had.'

Robin told him about fixing up Lilith's room, and he offered his help.

'I wonder what her colours are,' Robin mused. She asked Mathew about his mother, what she was like, and the little boy answered as he had before. "Zackly like you, but different, Ragsy.'

'A lot of help,' grinned Noel ... but Noel proved a lot of help to Robin.

They changed the room completely. Noel took out all the furniture and got to work with the paintbrush. Not having the time to send into town for new tins, he made do with some cans in the garage. The colour was a pleasant pale cream, which should suit a Lilith, Robin said.

'You think she'll be a lily, then?' Noel asked.

'But you're no Robin.' He looked down at Robin's clear gold skin, pinky-gold lips, streaked fair hair. No red robin there.

'I was called after the field flower,' Robin reminded him, 'but yes, I do think she'll be a lily with a name of Lilith.'

'Yet Mathew is a sturdy soul,' said Noel with affection. His unmistakable fondness for the boy continually surprised Robin; it seemed to go deeper than the accepted amiable tolerance that most people find in them for little ones. Robin looked quizzically at the manager, and, evidently becoming conscious of her regard, Noel looked back.

Abruptly he said: 'I was married, you know, Rob.'

'I didn't know.'

'Well' ... jerkily ... 'it was some nine years ago. 'There'... another pause ... 'was a boy.'

'Your son, Noel?'

'Yes.'

'Don't tell me if it makes you unhappy.'

He hunched one shoulder. 'It's all right,' he said. He

added: 'Now.'

'He would have been Pablo's . . . Mathew's age?'

'Yes.'

'What about his mother?'

'Ainsley was very delicate. She and the child — well—'

'They both died?'

'Yes.'

'I'm sorry, Noel.' It was all she could think to say. How inadequate were words, yet what else could you offer?

'Ainsley was never meant to weather the storm of life,' he said awkwardly. 'But she wanted all she could while she could and I—'

'When you haven't long it has to be for ever,' nodded Robin. 'I think you made her happy, Noel.'

'I hope I did. I pray I did. But why did I have to lose the child as well?'

'Better, perhaps.' Robin hated herself for the hackneyed comfort, yet again, what else could she say?

'So Mathew is now that boy?' she asked.

'Yes, Rob, to me he is young Ian.'

This time Robin touched his arm, not trusting herself with words.

Noel was not busy on the station at present, so he spent a lot of time on the room, Robin beside him, doing the less strenuous things, adding, she hoped, the woman's touch. They both enjoyed the job that they did together, their discussions on what was nearest both their hearts: the land. If anyone had overheard their conversation they would not have believed it was a man and a woman talking, and Robin said so ruefully one day, rather hoping that Noel would refute her words.

He didn't. He said cheerfully: 'You're a good sort, young Rob. And I've no doubt Tamar had that in view when he placed me here with you.'

'Had what in view?'

'V to M, as a matter of fact, based on our undoubted

compatibility.'

'View to Matrimony? Did he know about you and Ainsley, then?'

'He's always known us,' Noel said.

'He doesn't look a matchmaker.'

'He'd just have wanted my happiness, I expect.'

'But you didn't get it – I mean, not with me.'

'I got Mathew.' Noel's eyes were bright.

'Only for a while.'

'One never knows.' There was a soft note of hope.

But *I* know, Robin thought, I heard a man say: ' . . . I can't imagine how I ever thought of her as that,' and he had been referring to Lilith as a stepmother. Then he had said: 'She's far too young — Far too lovely.'

And with Lilith must go Mathew.

She wanted to comfort Noel, she wanted to say: 'Don't get hurt.'

But instead she brought the conversation back to the safety of Nooroo. Sheep. Pigs. Horses. Cotton-to-be.

'And sunflowers,' she urged. 'Noel, I've always wanted Nooroo to go in for sunflowers. Great big flowers with faces like clocks. Did you know that Anne of Cleves first heard of her betrothal to Henry VIII in a field of sunflowers?'

'It doesn't sound like him.'

'It was his ensign, I expect. But I can still see her there . . . she was small . . . completely dwarfed by the tall plants. Rows and rows of plants. The sunflowers of Cleves.'

'And I can see,' laughed Noel, 'that this pale cream room would never be for you. You're a typical sunflower girl, not a Lilith lily.'

Only he was wrong. They both were wrong. Lilith arrived the following afternoon.

And she was neither sunflower nor lily. She was a rose.

CHAPTER EIGHT

'A ROSE by any other name,' Robin was saying as she galloped Ribbons across the Red Plain. She and Jim always had called this dry-as-old-hay section to the north-west of Nooroo, and Yarani, the Red Plain, even though the authentic red plains did not open up properly for many miles yet. What else, the two children had claimed, could you name crimson flats reflecting back the sun's fire right to the distant sandstone hills?

Out here it was real cattle country – no wonder old Glenville had looked at it and seen a different kingdom from sheep. When he had switched, the others (including Grandfather) had sneered; their part of the west had always been sheep and they intended it to remain so. But, seeing a herd of thriving bullocks with their sleek mothers being driven into the fold of a nearer sandstone hill ... Robin raising her whip in distant acknowledgment and receiving a wave back ... she knew now that old Glenville had been right. Not entirely right, Yarani could still run sheep, but right enough to put Glenville on the winning side, particularly with the Brahma fellows, those humped Indian cattle that this climate suited equally well as Tamar Warren's 'balls of wool.' Robin's lip lifted at that derogatory description, or derogatory she chose to interpret it.

Ribbons, whose first enthusiasm over a gallop had diminished somewhat at feeling red earth and not grass any longer under her hooves, had slackened pace. It gave Robin more scope for contemplation. A rose, she thought of Mathew's mother again. Yes, Lilith would still have been a rose regardless.

As the other girl – for that was all she still was; her first marriage must have been in her teens, Mathew almost a little brother in comparative age instead of a son – had come up the path to where Noel and Robin had stood, Robin's heart had turned over in quick pain. She was so beautiful, not just pretty, not just that 'very young, very lovely' of Tamar's, but beautiful. It wasn't fair, Robin had thought, looking at the long black hair, the luminous dark eyes, the perfect creamy skin. She had been aware more than ever of her own sun-streaked locks, her blue eyes that she often suspected were beginning to fade out from too much looking into sun-flooded plains, her frankly freckled face.

Then, as though that was not enough, Lilith had been *sweet*. Not the assumed sweetness that must come easily when you are beautiful, but a true sweetness that was a instinctive as it was unmistakable.

When Mathew, seeing his mother, had raced forward, Robin's pain had been almost unbearable. All this, she had thought jealously, and Pablo, too. For undoubtedly the little boy's adoration was only equalled by his mother's devotion.

She had heard a faint noise at her side, a grunt, or a catch of a breath . . . or perhaps just a stir . . . and she had glanced at Noel. But he had stood there so implacably she had wondered had she imagined that small reaction. When Lilith had climbed the steps, a slim white hand extended, he had still stood stiff and apparently untouched. He had excused himself and left almost at once.

'He's not usually like that,' Robin had said of the manager. In case Lilith was hurt at the abrupt departure she had added: 'He did most of your room.'

'That was kind of him. And' . . . quickly, graciously . . . 'kind of you, too, for I think you did the rest.'

'I enjoyed it. Ever since I first saw Glenville' . . . Robin's cheeks had flushed and she had been sorry she had put herself into the position of admitting that she had never visited the adjoining homestead before . . . 'I've

118

felt Nooroo was badly in need of a new face.'

'A very lovely new face, this angle of it, anyway,' Lilith had said of the cream and gold bedroom she had been led to. 'How did you know my favourite colour scheme?'

'We thought of you as the same as your name.'

'A lily?'

'Yes.'

'But "we", you say? I mean, Tamar had already seen me in England.'

'Noel,' Robin murmured. 'I told you, he worked on the room.'

'Yes. Noel, of course. I've gathered from Mat's letters that my son is very keen on the manager.'

'That,' Robin had informed her, 'is rather an understatement. Will you come now and have tea?'

'It would be lovely,' assented Lilith.

At once she and Mrs. MacPherson had been firm friends. She had praised the little cakes the cook had brought out, not praised them as Robin would have done by simply coming back for more, but asking for her recipe as well, *really* asking for it, not just being polite.

'You're a cook yourself, Mrs. Warren?' Mrs. Mac had asked.

'I try to be. I do like it.'

Robin had fidgeted in her chair. It had not helped her that Tamar Warren by this time had been present also for tea. He had arrived soon after Lilith, and he had sat on the opposite side of the table to Robin, looking at her with that faint amusement that so infuriated her.

I suppose, Robin had thought unhappily, on top of everything else Lilith will prove the perfect country girl, will put me to shame there, too. But Lilith wasn't. Also she didn't pretend to be. Instead she stepped down so graciously, so generously, that being better at that was no triumph at all. Robin now dug in her heels, and Ribbons, who had settled down to a lazy pace, responded rather resentfully. Two querulous girls, admitted Robin ruefully.

As she turned Ribbons back to the homestead she found herself musing, as she had several times before, on Noel's reaction to the lovely girl who had come among them. For it had been nil. No withdrawal, which at least would have been positive and given rise to a suspicion that Noel himself was anything but withdrawn, but simply nothing. Lilith on her side had been equally non-committal. Only Pablo had shown any enthusiasm.

'Now we're the family,' he had claimed, not at all discouraged when no one took him up on that.

A week had gone by since then, a week of Lilith settling in . . . she had confided to Robin that she wanted to stay put a while before she started to move again . . . a week of Noel still staging that polite uninterest, a week of Tamar Warren showing a lot of interest . . . and a week of Robin waiting for her marching orders. For there was no reason at all now for her to stay on at Nooroo.

Robin had given Tamar back the engagement ring, and he had shrugged as he had accepted it.

'No need really,' he had said.

'Please take it.'

'Yarani is a very easygoing place, they wouldn't care if you didn't keep on earning it,' he had nodded to the slender circlet.

'I don't want it,' she insisted.

'Please yourself, then.' He had put the ring in his pocket.

So she was not needed in that department, Robin had thought, just as in Noel's department, for a young jackeroo had been signed on, and he was proving himself very efficient. When Robin found herself cut out of a boundary job one morning she said aloud: 'I may as well offer myself to Mrs. Mac as a dishwasher.'

'Except that I've installed an electric one.' Tamar happened to have ridden up in time to hear Robin. 'Why not sit on the verandah some time and polish your nails?'

She had glanced quickly down at her nails, square on her small capable brown hands, and, fortunately, very clean at the moment, for, working as she did, they could more often be dirty. Clean dirt, Grandfather Mansfield had always claimed.

'Like Lilith does?' she had asked.

'Why not?'

'Because I'm still being paid a salary and presumably Lilith isn't.' Her teeth had clipped down on her bottom lip, a habit of Robin's. Not paid, she thought of Lilith, unless you counted V to M as payment. View to . . . what a silly phrase! Why couldn't they say plain intention?

'Thinking it over, leave them natural,' advised Tamar.

'The nails?'

'What else?'

'How long more will you be requiring me, Mr. Warren?' She had no need to address him as Tamar any more and evidently he concurred with this because he never, now, corrected her.

'You're anxious to go?'

'Naturally I'm anxious about my future.'

'How do you mean, naturally?'

'I'm unmarried, and it's usual for unmarried people to be concerned about their next post.'

'Your brother and sister-in-law wouldn't see you stuck,' he said smoothly.

'It's not the usual thing to inflict yourself upon newly-weds,' she answered stiffly, a lot of her stiffness because of what she was reluctantly thinking. I think Jim and Ginny wouldn't care at all, she was facing up.

'I'll let you know.' He said it abruptly, but the impact on Robin had not been his abruptness but the fact that he was now ready to relinquish her. Previously he had found reasons to hold on to her, solely for the assistance she could give, of course, assistance that was obviously no longer necessary following the arrival of Lilith for Mathew, the jackaroo for Noel. She was expendable, Robin had accepted ... but still finding it hard to accept it from him.

The homestead was in sight now, no more red plain and dry-as-old-hay underfoot covering. Although the grass at Nooroo was never really lush, not like the southern districts with their bigger rainfalls, it seemed lush now in comparison, and Ribbons let her head go, and Robin permitted her.

As they cantered up to the homestead verandah, Robin saw that Tamar had come again. Instead of saying as she always did: 'Why not? It's his,' she said, privately of course: 'Why not? Lilith's here.'

Lilith was not here at the moment, though, but a very excited little boy was.

'Ragsy ... in moments of excitement Mathew forgot their pact and called Robin that ... 'I'm going, too.'

For a minute she thought he meant going away, but Tamar came in smoothly, 'He means he's included.'

'In what?'

'To see the wild horses,' Mathew explained. 'Even perhaps' ... a glance at Tamar ... 'get one.'

'I told you, sonno, that's very improbable. If you were free would you like to be cooped up?'

'Maryann and Maryjane aren't cooped up,' pointed out Mathew. They were the new fillies and they were decidedly not confined, they had all the far northern field to themselves.

'It's different,' pointed out Tamar, 'from a whole wide world, or so a wild horse must think.'

'But you still said if one wanted to come—'

'Yes, I said that, but don't bank on it.'

'What is all this?' came in Robin. 'It sounds like a wild

herd has been sighted.'

'Past the Ten Mile,' Tamar told her. 'The last time a mob was seen out of Yarani—'

'Was in my Grandfather's time,' came in Robin.

'Also mine,' he reminded her.

'Did your grandfather tell you about it?' she asked a little breathlessly, for to Robin it had been one of the most breathless stories Grandfather had had to tell.

'Yes,' he said, just a Yes, but she could feel his thrall, too. So he had felt like she had felt.

Tamar said, 'If possible I'd like the kid to have that thrill.'

She nodded mutely ... she seemed beyond words. But she did manage to ask: 'When are we going? That is' ... remembering she had not yet been invited, only included by Mathew ... 'if I—'

'You're coming, too.'

'And Noel?'

'Yes, the jack. Some of the Glenville boys. We may even get one of the brumby stragglers, who knows?'

'You won't push it that way, though?' she asked anxiously. Although she had never seen a mob running, she could imagine it ... but she could not imagine a prisoner.

'No, I won't push it,' he promised quite kindly, kind considering she had no right to ask.

'Is Lilith coming?' Lilith had been taking riding lessons from Tamar and seemed to be doing very well.

'She wouldn't be up to it yet. The mob was seen out of the Ten Mile, as I said. If we left in the morning and took a roundabout track when we got close in case the fellows got wind of us, we should be in time for any late afternoon watering, which should be at that hole beyond the Ten Mile.'

'I know,' Robin nodded. She did know that hole, it lay at the dent between two hills; to reach it the horses would have to come over one of the hills. She held her breath for a moment at the imagined sight of them.

'It mightn't be like that at all.' His voice cut in laconically, and she knew he had been aware what she had been dreaming. Aware again.

'Ribbons up to the distance?' he asked next.

'Yes.' She said it a little uncertainly in spite of her eagerness, for it was a long way and the filly a rather delicate fine type for hard lengthy treks. However, if Pablo was doing it on his little mount—

'Mathew is going in the Glenville jeep as far as the Ten Mile.' Again he had read her. 'After that either you or I or someone can take him in front of them. How about the new fellow, Miss Mansfield? Feel you can handle him' ... a pause ... 'this time?'

'I handled him last time.'

'But arrived at a different destination,' he reminded her unkindly. 'The mob was seen out of the Ten Mile, not Retreat Creek.'

'I would like that,' she admitted humbly. 'Ribbons is a perfect mount, but she is – well—'

'Take Chief, then.'

'Is that his name?' After Maryann and Maryjane it sounded very ambitious.

'Chief Glenville,' he said smoothly. He looked challengingly at her. 'Why not?'

'Why not?' she agreed. Well – why not? Old Glenville had been chief of Yarani.

'I'm glad we're in agreement,' he said a little too smoothly. 'By the way,' as she turned to go inside, 'no need to worry about direction, I've cured the bay of that.' He said it confidently, in the manner of one used to curing inadequacies in people. He had even cured her inadequacy of being unable to ride in Lilith. But, thought Robin triumphantly, he has cured nothing in me. She glanced round and saw that he was regarding her with estimation. At any moment, she thought, he'll say with that horrible intuition of his: 'Oh, yes, but I *will*.'

Tamar Warren didn't. At least not aloud.

They took off early the next day, as Tamar had planned. The sun was up, but barely so, shadows still clustered in the folds of the distant hills. That sense of expectancy that dawn always holds had not quite vanished. It silenced Mathew as he watched the departure, as he waited for the Glenville jeep that would take him by the track to the Ten Mile, and when he spoke it was in a small rapt voice to Robin.

'It's exciting, Ragsy.'

'Yes, Pablo.'

The horses, too, seemed to feel the hushed wonder, and they went silently away from Nooroo.

Tamar had come earlier on his own mount and towing Chief. He had legged Robin up and given the stallion a little slap as he said: 'Behave yourself today.'

'The horse or the rider?' Robin had asked impudently; this man always raised a devil in her.

'The horse got the smack,' he reminded her, and he got to the front and started the string across the Mitchell grass, which would later give way to red earth, Robin knew.

Yarani was on the final fringe, that fringe between the plains and the desert. Besides what man had given it, and that was ground cover and sheep (and now cattle) to feed from the ground cover, there was what man had not given – the clay pans, the salt pans, the rock outcrop, an occasional patch of gibber. Kangaroos. Brumby camels. Purple patches of Salvation Jane.

But it was the wild horses they sought.

It was not usual for the horses to come so far south, to travel so far eastward; the last time any had been around here was over half a century ago. But the long dry must have set the horses seeking fodder, and they had been sighted several times making for the hole out of the Ten

Mile. It was probable the two sightings would be all they would afford anyone, but Robin hoped she would see them, hoped Mathew would, for it would be an unforgettable experience.

Chief was behaving beautifully, showing off his long springy stride, but never once putting a foot in front of the leader, Tamar's mount.

'Not quite the chief,' Robin observed drily of Tamar's mount's precedence.

'The chief of a lesser kingdom, perhaps,' Tamar suggested. 'We'll have smoko round that next hill.'

Like all the 'hills' here, you had to be used to the country to mark any rise, but Robin was long accustomed, and she knew that Tamar was not referring to the sandstone slopes in the distance, now taking on the butter yellow of day, but the tiny inclines much nearer to them, almost mere saucer rims.

'Where do we meet Pab— Mathew?' she inquired.

'The jeep will take him to the track end, then he can travel in front of me. I think this will do for our billy.' As he spoke, Tamar swung himself from the saddle, leaving Robin to dismount herself.

'Don't stand around, rustle up some tinder,' he said to the rest of the string . . . and to Robin. She brought her share of twigs and dry leaves and in a few minutes a fire was burning in a small ring of stones he had formed, stones being easy to come by out here. In the way that only bushmen can, he coaxed a fire that began almost at once to boil the water he had emptied from a waterbag. Robin had seen it done often, but never ceased wondering about it, wondering at the ease the flame responded, almost like turning on a gas jet. In no time Tamar was swinging the billy in a circle to let the brew draw, and then he was pouring out the black-gold liquid, fragrant as no other drink is fragrant, thought Robin, no other beverage ever could compare with bush billy tea.

She must have said it aloud, for, oblivious of the string of riders now squatted on their haunches around them, either oblivious or not caring, he asked: 'Not even wedding champagne?'

'I've never had it.'

'On your own accord, no, but your brother's surely?'

'Ginny and Jim were married very quietly. Jim is a reticent person, and Ginny ... well, she was scarcely in that mood.'

'For champagne or marriage?'

'She was at the end of an affair,' Robin said stiffly.

'Surely a call for dancing bubbles,' he suggested laconically.

'A long affair,' Robin replied coldly. 'She waited, and then ...' She shrugged.

'Did Ginny tell you that?' he asked sharply, but in her noting how once again he had called her sister-in-law Ginny, just as he had called Pat Pat, Lilith Lilith, familiar with everyone, it seemed, save Robin, Robin did not catch the sharpness.

'I'll stick to tea,' she said positively.

'You should try sugar in it some time,' he suggested blandly, and she knew he was referring to her, not the tea.

She got to her feet and went across to Chief. He was a tall horse to mount, but she remembered this and made an extra effort. To her annoyance, she did not quite make it. She had a second go, and managed to get astride just as Tamar strolled across.

'You ought to grow up a bit, Miss Mansfield.'

'I'm on, aren't I?'

'Yes, you're on. If I mistook you I would still not mistake the voice. You try that sugar.'

'Put in someone's mouth to lead him where I want to go?'

He had not moved away from Chief. He looked up at her and his eyes were very direct. 'Could be he wanted to

127

go, too?' he suggested.

While she searched for a pert answer he climbed his own mount and headed the string once more towards the west.

The sun was beating down now. Because it was a long time since she had taken a ride like this, Robin had not thought to bring a fly veil. She pretended she was not annoyed by the persistent little bush variety that kept brushing her forehead, but when Tamar handed over a veil she was too grateful to be resentful that he had remembered and she had not.

Chief was impatient to move and he fidgeted restlessly when she pulled him up so she could adjust the veil over her hat. Tamar came across and did it for her, his eyes flicking at hers through the two layers of fly mesh, for he had pulled his over, too. But, as it could be out here, within a mile there were no flies. They were climbing a little, climbing up a saucer rim. The Ten Mile, Robin remembered, should be the other side of the top.

No one knew why it was the Ten Mile, whether it was ten miles to somewhere, or from somewhere. But for years a track had gone there, gone to nowhere, and as they reached the rim top they saw the station jeep below with a Glenville driver and Mathew.

They had more tea, with sandwiches this time, tea that the driver had fetched in flasks, then Tamar took Mathew up in front of him, and they began their undefined journey into the bush.

'No need to tell you not to wander,' Tamar tossed to Robin, and Robin nodded. The terrain looked innocuous enough, it seemed quite open and friendly, but turn round a different rock, brush past a different tree, and you could be lost for hours. A day. – Forever. The earliest lesson you learned out here was not to take location lightly, and Robin saw to it she kept with the rest, and even then marked her way.

An hour after they had left the Ten Mile something happened to assure them ... if sadly ... that the wild ones had come through these parts.

It was Mathew who saw the little fellow first, which was not surprising, really, Robin thought; even a baby will focus a child before an adult will. The call of the young to the young ... except that one of these two young ones could never call back.

The little newly born foal lying on the ground was apparently fast asleep. But he was dead.

Tamar's glance said this to Robin as she began to veer Chief towards the seemingly pretty little scene – a mother, for the mare was standing by, watching her baby while it slept. But Robin knew from Tamar's look, it would be a long sleep.

They went on, Mathew openly complaining that he had not been availed the opportunity to get off and see the small fellow.

'We've come for something else,' reminded Tamar rather shortly, and he passed Mathew on to Smithers, who was riding a big grey. He got into stride beside Robin.

'Better not to upset him, I think.'

'Yes,' she agreed. She was quiet a while. Then: 'I don't like the foal left out like that, though.'

'It has to be,' said Tamar, 'for the mother's sake. She'll never accept him as dead until she's convinced that he can't get up. If we took the poor little thing away now, she would become upset, believe it had wandered away when she wasn't looking, then begin to search.'

'She'll accept it now?'

'In her own good time,' Tamar nodded.

'How would it happen? I mean, the mother looks fit. I think to be wild out here you would need to be fit.'

'I agree. All I can hazard is that the small one was presented upside down at birth, and smothered.'

'What will happen to the mother?'

'She'll rejoin the mob. That's one thing we've learned, anyway, from this little interlude. The horses are definitely around.' Tamar glanced across at Mathew, sitting astride, in front of Bill Smithers. He had forgotten his resentment at not being able to go across to the foal. And better this way, Robin found herself approving ... approving perhaps for her first time of Tamar Warren; children did not comprehend death, it had to be taught to them, and Mathew was too young, and today was not the day.

It also did not seem the day for the horses. They had gone on some miles more, stopped for tea, Mathew had been given to another rider, the waterhole had been reached and circled several times, but it appeared they were not going to appear, when—

It was Chief who first alerted Robin. He began sniffing, drawing in long eager breaths, and wonderingly Robin drew Tamar's attention to this. Tamar watched the bay, noted the rise of his head, heard the soft half whinny.

'Do you know,' he said excitedly, 'I do believe Chief has known all this before.'

'All what?'

'Old days, old ways, old stretches, old haunts. My God, he could even have belonged!'

'But you bought him.'

'Catalogue bought, and no sire or dam named. He could have been one of the wild ones. – Watch it, Robin!' The last came out sharply, bullet sharp, but it was too late. Without any warning, the bay was leaping instinctively forward, racing upward, and over, conquering the many uneven patches as though he flew, not raced. As though he was winged.

'He *is* one of them.' That was the first thing that Robin said, and with it, in spite of her sheer terror at being borne, flown, she could have said, over the rough hill, she knew a fierce kind of joy, yet a pain with it, the sweet pain of returning where you belonged. She felt it for Chief.

'Hold on!' Tamar's voice came screaming at her from somewhere to the rear, but in the unreality the sound was blurred, unreal.

She heard it, though, and she called back: 'I can't. I can't!' For the pace was augmenting now, the ground growing rougher, Robin was grabbing at Chief with her hands, her knees, all of her, but still she knew it could not be for long.

'I'm coming!' he called.

By the time his voice reached her, he reached her. She had the vague sensation of a hand reaching out, and she thought it would be for her rein.

'Break clear!' This time the order was so staccato there was no blur, no hazy wonder about it. At once Robin obeyed. Then, the instant her feet cleared the stirrups, she felt herself being lifted out of the saddle, being deposited, as Mathew had been, in front of the man. The big horse Tamar rode was pulled up, then Robin was lowered to the ground. The man came after her.

'I don't know what happened—' Robin began, but he stopped her.

'Look,' he said.

Staring upward, further down the hill the rest of their string staring up, too, Mathew also staring, they saw something that is given to very few to see, even a very few in the west. The wild horses were running.

No one knew from where they had come, but it could be a long way from here. No one knew why, they could only guess, but what they all did know was that it was something that they would never forget. The ground where they stood was trembling, up there it would be like the waves of an earthquake. But it was the sight of the horses that was the unforgettable thing. All those dilated

131

nostrils, those flowing manes. It was a big bunch, but it went past like a sequence in a dream.

And when it had gone right by, it was a big bunch *plus more*.

Chief had joined the wild mob.

CHAPTER NINE

'WILL you get the saddle back?' Mathew, in front of Simpson, was asking Tamar ... a Tamar now with Robin in front of him.

Quite noticeably Robin had stepped back when it had come to remounting after the wild bunch had raced past, after the ground had stopped trembling, after Tamar, since she had no horse now, had nodded indicatively to the space in front of him.

Probably annoyed with her hesitancy in front of the men, Tamar had said for her ears alone and very sharply: 'Climb up at once, please. It will only be as far as the track, thank heaven. You can go home with the young 'un in the jeep then.'

Still she had paused, and only that quick anger in his eyes had changed her mind. This man, she knew, wouldn't mind what kind of spectacle he made, or she made, of himself, of herself, so long as he imposed his will. She had obeyed, and a minute afterwards he had swung himself up behind her. Anyone who has ever ridden with someone else on a mount know there can be few closer human contacts than two on one horse. Shrink as she tried, Robin still sat as near to Tamar Warren as anyone could sit near to someone. She even felt his breath warm down the back of her neck. Once when his horse leapt a cleft in the rocks, she was forced to steady herself by placing her hands tightly over his.

'I should have put you at the back,' he said with cool amusement, 'you could have clung, not hung, then.'

She did not answer. It was bad enough to hold on to his hand, but to encircle his big middle with both arms would have been the very end.

'Will you?' persisted Mathew now of Tamar, 'will you ever get the saddle back, do you think?'

'Not unless Chief comes along one day and hands it in.' A speculative pause. 'Which could happen.'

It was just too much for Robin. This man had gone to watch the wild horses, and if any of them was readily available to avail himself of it, but what was the position now? He had lost, not won, a horse.

She commented of his succinct: 'Which could happen' a scornful: 'And pigs might fly.'

Mathew, always factual, said reproachfully, 'Ragsy, pigs don't fly.'

Tamar repeated solidly, ignoring Robin's scorn, 'Which could happen. Chief has had the taste of a feed-bag twice a day, the comfort of shelter, the touch of gentle hands.' He touched Robin's, away from his now, derisively. 'Even the wind in his mane might not be worth that loss.'

'No,' agreed Mathew hopefully, 'and none of the horses greeted him, did they? I think they didn't even know him. So he could come back.'

'It probably wasn't his own bunch, sonno,' pointed out Tamar of the lack of greeting, 'it was another bunch altogether. I feel that Chief was rounded up a long way from here, and even though this lot came from a long way, too, more likely than not they were not his relations or friends. I think all that Chief recognized was old ways, old days.' He paused, then went on: 'Old calls. But who knows? Another call might come.'

'And your saddle come along with it?' Robin questioned too blandly.

'No,' he said, pretending to take her seriously, 'it would fall off during the flight, and even if it didn't I hardly think he would return it in his mouth like a dog a ball.'

'If he returns,' she stuck out.

'Sometimes you do come back,' Tamar said. He pulled his mount up so abruptly that she lurched forward. 'Off,'

he said without grace. 'You can ride the rest of the way.'
He nodded to the waiting jeep.

'I have ridden,' she retorted.

'You'll be more comfortable now, I think.'

'Yes, I think that, too.' She slid off, collected Mathew
from Simpson and the pair joined the jeep, which had
been reversed ready for the return trip. The horses
formed a string once more and were soon lost in the long-
eared grass.

They were home hours before the riders, and Lilith
was told the thrilling story of the horses by a breathless
Mathew.

'Chief remembered old ways, old days,' related Lilith's
son from Tamar, 'so he went with the wild ones, and now
he has wind in his mane, only you don't forget feedbags
and shelter and ... what else was it, Ragsy?'

'I forget.'

'You can't. It was when Tamar put his hands on
yours.'

Robin, painfully aware of flushing cheeks and Lilith's
glance on her, said: 'That was to steady myself when we
leapt over that rock.'

'It was the touch of gentle hands,' recalled Mathew
with triumph. 'So you see, Mummy, Chief could come
back.'

'Not a chance,' dismissed Robin. She tossed to Lilith:
'Briefly, we not only didn't get what we went after, we lost
in the trying.'

'Oh, Robin!' said Mathew. When he called her that she
knew he was annoyed with her. She watched him march
out, then said a little defensively to his mother: 'Well, it's
true.'

'I think I'll be on Mat's side and say Chief could come
back.'

'Well, one thing, I won't be here to see that miracle.'
Robin left that open, waiting for Lilith to add her intention, too, to depart.

Lilith didn't.

Mrs. MacPherson had brought in tea, and the two girls sat together drinking it. A little guiltily, Robin said: 'I didn't mean to dash Mathew down, Lilith.'

'You were wise,' assured Mathew's mother, 'to prepare him for something that probably won't happen. I'm rather surprised at Mathew thinking it would, he's quite a factual child. But I suppose Tamar saying it ...' She shrugged.

Robin, on the verge of telling Lilith that anything said by *Noel* would carry even more import, refrained. Already she had said too much, she chided herself.

'He's practical, yet practical with a dream,' she remarked instead of the little boy.

'As was his father.'

There was a little silence.

'How long ago?' Robin asked gently of the young mother.

'Since Gene, you mean? Gene died before Mathew was born.'

'And you never—'

'No,' came in Lilith.

Robin had meant to finish 'And you never married until you married Tamar's father?' Lilith's quick insertion made the completion of the question unnecessary.

The riders were coming up the drive. Robin saw that the Glenville crowd was still with the Nooroo, so evidently the posse had come back the same way as it had gone. She told Mrs. MacPherson to brew more tea, but that efficient lady already had done so, had fixed a large batch of scones. As the men rested on the verandah, drank, munched and yarned, Tamar Warren caught Robin's glance. Wearing that baiting smile of his, he deliberately held up one of the scones.

Chief was not replaced. The local horse was brought in and put in a paddock near the two fillies.

'Which one will Nightcap like, do you think?' asked

Mathew of Noel.

'Will they like him is more important, sonno.'

'I'm sure they will.'

'You can't ever be sure,' Noel said rather shortly, or so Robin thought. She wondered . . .

A second jackeroo had arrived. Wattie had been allotted a help. A dam-building team was starting on a declination that Tamar had marked as a suitable water storage site. Nooroo was growing up at last.

Though she tried to resent every change, in her heart Robin knew they were long overdue.

'Grandfather,' she told him in her weekly letter, 'would have been proud of the place . . . except, of course, that it's sprung from a Glenville source. I expect you'll be seeing me quite soon, brother, there's so much staff here you get lost in the crowd. So different from the sparse old days. I'm sure it won't be long, for I know I'm not needed any more.'

When she said this to Tamar on one of his visits, being anxious to get in first and leave before she was told to, he replied calmly: 'I'll tell you when.'

'I can go when I like, and don't say to me that I won't go because of Nooroo, because it isn't Nooroo, not *my* Nooroo, any more.'

'You don't like efficiency?'

'I like the old place.'

He raised pitying brows, yet did not comment, but he did say: 'I wasn't going to tell you that.'

She waited. She saw from his expression he had not finished.

'I was going to tell you that you can't go, though not because of any sentimental reasons but because of the fine print,' he said formally.

'What fine print?'

'Remember signing a form?'

She did, though rather vaguely; she had thought it was the usual easygoing agreement they adopted out here.

'There was a little stipulation,' he smiled hatefully, 'a matter of you *having* to remain for six months.'

'I don't *have* to do anything.'

'Or forfeit a sum of money,' he finished blandly.

'You're impossible!' she gasped.

'And you're imprudent, not looking through the thing first, or having someone do it for you.'

'I trust people,' Robin snapped.

'Then don't.'

When Jim's letter came he did not even mention Nooroo, which was not so surprising, he never had been interested. But the really disturbing part of the letter was his '. . . about seeing you soon, Rob – well, that will be good – though what happened to something I thought was going to happen and hasn't? You must tell me when you come down, though not, I'm afraid, under this roof. For certain reasons, old girl, you'll have to find your own roof.'

So the split had begun . . . or was beginning soon! For that was what Jim must mean. If everything had been right, they would have wanted her.

Robin rang Sydney that night, and as she waited to be connected she wondered miserably what to say. Ginny answered the call and they went through the usual how-are-you exchanges.

Then Robin cleared her throat and said: 'Ginny.'

'Robin?'

'In his letter Jim hinted – well, I mean he half insinuated—'

Ginny waited.

'He always was serious over what he said,' Robin said next, 'and that's why—'

It was a bad connection. Robin could barely hear her sister-in-law. Apart from that she could not speak out as she wanted to, not with possibly half a dozen people listening to her on the party line.

'I'll write,' she said desperately. 'But, Ginny, please be

sure. Be quite sure.'

'We are,' Ginny called, but the conversation had to end
there.

Robin was standing on the verandah staring unhappily
out when Tamar came up the drive.

'A penny,' he said carelessly.

She did not parry with him, she said abruptly: 'I want
to leave.'

'Have you that money I told you about, then?'

'You know I haven't.'

'Then don't waste my time.'

'It's important,' she insisted.

'So is that clause, which I would act on, and don't have
two thoughts about my meaning that, Miss Mansfield.'

'Why,' she asked on a sudden impulse and a little
angrily, 'do you always call me Miss Mansfield?'

'I didn't always,' he reminded her.

'That was for a purpose.'

'A purpose that is no longer needed,' he agreed.

'But now you've returned to Miss Mansfield.'

'Your name, isn't it?'

'Pat was Pat, Lilith is Lilith, Ginny—'

She became aware that he was looking at her narrowly
now. 'And why is Ginny in this?' he demanded.

'Because you call her that, yet—'

'Yet I call you Miss Mansfield? What would you
prefer? Darling?'

She did not reply to that, she said, returning stubbornly
to her former subject: 'I'm not needed here at Nooroo
any more.'

'I told you that I'll be the judge of that. And I judge
that I do need you a little longer yet.'

'Because of Lilith?'

'So you've guessed that?'

'Of course,' Robin said. After a while she burst out:
'Now that Mrs. MacPherson is here, I could go.'

'I agree there's no longer any need for you as a second

woman, but I feel Lilith could do with your younger company. Your presence, anyway, in what I plan next week. Lilith has expressed a wish to see more of this country. I thought she might like the Palisades.'

'That's a long way away,' Robin reminded him.

'Yes.'

'It entails a stop.'

'Several, to do it comfortably.'

'And you want me as a third?'

'No,' he said quite indifferently, 'as a fourth. I would like another man. A journey that far out calls for another man. If nothing else it would even us up. Noel would do, I think.'

'Can he be spared?'

'I would be doing any sparing since I'm—'

'You're the boss.'

'Exactly. You're learning at last, Miss Mansfield.' His eyes flicked at her. 'Anyway, why shouldn't Noel rush it? A couple of days away from work with two beautiful girls.'

'Thank you.'

'Well, I didn't like to leave you out.'

'Is this,' Robin asked after a long seething pause, 'an order?'

'An order,' he agreed.

'For Noel and for me?'

'Exactly. For Lilith, it's an invitation.'

'I see.'

'That's all you have to do, see that you comply.'

'And Noel?'

'Leave his compliance to me, please.'

Without waiting for any comment, Tamar went into the house . . . well, why not, it was his house . . . calling: 'Lilith . . . Lilith . . . hi there, Mrs. Warren, how does this appeal?'

Robin ran down the steps away from the house. Mrs. Warren, she heard again, but said, of course, in fun, for

Lilith was always Lilith to Tamar. Said in a totally different strain from his 'Miss Mansfield', which was never said in fun. Mrs. Warren, Robin thought again, who was going to be yet another Mrs. Warren. But how could Tamar marry the wife of the father he had obviously adored? How could he?

Mathew joined her, and as they went down to inspect some lettuce that Wattie had let the little boy plant, it came to Robin that although she had written Mathew down as a pupil in her old school attendance book, she had not known his name, she had simply put Mathew Warren for convenience.

'Darling, what's your name?' she asked now.

'You know it. Pablo.'

'No, not that, and not Mathew, either.'

'John,' said Mathew. Then: 'Mathew John Warren.'

'But Pab, a man always keeps his own name.' That seemed a better explanation to Robin than saying that in the second marriage of a child's mother, the child does not take the other name.

'Warren,' repeated Mathew, 'and my first name is Rabbit.' He was delighted with his pun, and refused to be serious, so Robin dropped the subject. After all, why should he be serious? Why should anyone be serious? She remembered Jim's serious letter. Ginny's serious voice over the phone.

Oh, no, Robin thought, let's not be serious.

No one knew why their outcrop of rocks to the west had been named the Palisades. Certainly the balancing piles seemed to divide the red west from the less red, less western Yarani district, but there was nothing fence-like in the irregular blocks thrown around the top of the only visible hill.

No one knew, either, how they had got there. Scientists sometimes came out to look for Permian occurrences in them, but, apart from these men, the outcrop, being less spectacular than other more publicized rocks, was deserted, and still looked, Robin thought thankfully, the same as she remembered it from that time she and Grandfather had ridden out, many many years ago now.

The colouring was unbelievable. The collection of irregular stones would be violet one minute, a flame of red the next. Every time you turned to take another look a new aspect awaited you. Because the day was ending now ... they had ridden since early morning ... Arabian Nights hues were taking over, deep blues, glowing purples, old pottery golds.

Lilith was thrilled. She pulled up the mount she had ridden very well ... and very uncomplainingly for a new rider tackling her first all day journey, and gazed wonderingly across.

'It's unbelievable,' she murmured.

They were to camp there for the night, explore the next day, hit the trail for home on the third day. Tamar had selected a suitable stopover and already he and Noel were rigging the tents. It was the girls' duty to gather the wood for the fire, and knowing Tamar's impatience by now, though he would never be that, Robin thought, with Lilith, Robin began hurrying around.

Wood was scarce out here, you really had to search for it. Seeing a small copse some fifty yards away, Robin went across. She pulled out a few old mallee roots that should burn well, then looked around for something lighter for starting tinder. There was a windswept waste of leaves and twigs under the stunted trees, and, kneeling down, Robin extended her hand, then stopped. Within reach, though no snake needs to be that, for he has a long striking power, the small unimportant-looking reptile was curled up, but it was not unimportant, and Robin was acutely aware of that; it was venomous, and it could be fatal.

The reptile was somewhere between sleep and waking. At this hour these things awoke to take their nightly watering. Grandfather had fixed a hide for Robin when he had brought her out all those years ago, and, besides wallabies, lizards, bush rats, she had seen snakes come to drink. Just now she was all right, the thing was half drowsy and a little stupid still, but the least noise would arouse it, arouse it to the vigorous extent and intent one must expect after a long day's rest, and these little desert fellows were very quick to their mark. Quietly, with infinite care, Robin withdrew her hand, but she did not dare to withdraw herself.

Back at the camp she could hear voices, but she did not permit herself to look round. The snake's eyes were opening, and, as they always did, focusing. But he was not moving. Yet.

'Robin!' It was Lilith's voice behind her. Opening her lips as narrowly as she could to frame the two words, Robin said sharply: 'Go back!'

Lilith was intelligent, Robin knew, but she was also a newchum, she couldn't be expected to understand anything like this.

The eyes were quite open now and still focused on her. Go back, Lilith, Robin called in her mind. She *willed* Lilith to retreat.

And Lilith did. Afterwards she was to admit she did not know why she did so; she saw no snake, she saw nothing except Robin in the crouched position. But there must have been something that had warned her, for she had retreated, then run, run to the men.

It seemed a lifetime afterwards, though probably it was only seconds, that Robin heard the rustle at the other side of the small scrub. The snake heard it, too, undoubtedly he was intended to, for with almost incredible rapidity he disappeared. There seemed nowhere to disappear to, but camouflaged as he was in his desert-coloured skin, he could have merely moved his position a few inches yet escaped discovery. Not that Tamar wanted to discover him.

'It may be unheroic of me,' he said afterwards, 'but I wasn't feeling like doing any brave acts. Besides, they're a very tricky type.'

At the time he had called: 'Get back, Robin, get back fast!' He had retreated from his side and come round in time to swing her further back still.

'Look next time,' he said as they went back to the camp. 'Look like hell, you female clot!'

She barely heard him, she was thinking: 'He called out Robin, not Miss Mansfield, he called me by my name.'

'Clot's the right word,' Tamar was still fuming, 'but for Lilith's cool head—'

'And warm heart.' Robin found she could speak at last. The incident had unnerved her in spite of herself, and she tacked on a little hysterically: 'Isn't that so? Her warm heart?'

'It is,' answered Tamar Warren. 'Or at least that's what I'm hoping for.'

They reached the encampment and Lilith pushed a cup of sweet black tea into Robin's hand.

'The sugar for shock,' she advised.

'Not for sweetness?' Now Robin was fully recovered, and she looked at Tamar deliberately. 'You advised that, remember?'

'I still do, Miss Mansfield,' he said. Miss Mansfield, not Robin again. Not even, Robin thought, and found herself not far from hysterical laughter, Clot.

Noel had blue smoke trailing in the air now, the smoke that said it was time to throw on the steaks.

Lilith proved a good cook outside a house as well as in ... she had relieved Mrs. MacPherson on several occasions ... and while Noel attended to the big T-bones sizzling over the red embers, Mathew's mother wrapped potatoes in foil, did marvels with eggs and thick slabs of bacon in a blackened skillet.

But it was Tamar who finally, after the food was eaten,

brewed, then whirled round the billy. After the last drop of the dark golden tea was drained, the fire was built up, for the breezes even in summer could come with a chilly edge in the interior, and Noel and Tamar shared a small flask of rum, always the man's drink at campfires, and the girls were surprised by an apple wine from the Glenville cellars that Tamar had brought along.

'Though I've no doubt,' he drawled, 'Miss Mansfield has coped with overproof before, she tells me she used to come west with her grandfather on safaris like this, and a safari just isn't one without a drop of the blood of Nelson.'

'There was no rum,' Robin said coolly.

'Then it's just as well I brought the wine,' he smiled, 'you could have made a fool of yourself.'

'Clot was the word.' On an impulse Robin leaned forward and took the bottle from Noel. The long gulp she grabbed proved fiery and horrible. She began to cough. Noel took the bottle back and he and Lilith laughed. But Tamar Warren said coldly: 'What were we talking about?'

'Grandfather Mansfield,' called Robin recklessly. 'Old Yarani.'

Noel had discreetly taken out a mouth organ and was beginning a tune. Lilith began singing to it in a sweet small voice. This was the time that campfire stories should be told, western sagas begin. There should be magical pauses when the moon looked down, when only bush things stirred, when the wood pheasants called gently their 'Move over, dear, move over, dear.' When the whole world stopped, or at least you felt you had imprisoned the navy blue perfection of it in the hollow of your hand. But alas! Robin was sick.

She stole away from the fire just in time, and there among the frogs, the small shiny beetles and ground things that had retreated from the circles of light, she was very unglamorously ill. It was the rum, she knew.

'Such a fine steak, too.' It was Tamar behind Robin.
'And those jacketed spuds.'

'Go away, please!'

'And those bacon and eggs.'

'*Please*, Tamar!'

To her surprise, if there was room for surprise in those
spasms, he said, 'Yes, Miss Mansfield,' and left.

Some time later Robin went exhaustedly to her sleeping mat.

Lilith awoke her with her excitement over a flock of budgerigar. Tumbling out of the small tent, Robin saw the
lovely young mother in her short yellow gown, a yellow
ribbon tying back her long dark hair. She was pointing
excitedly to the many whirring wings of bright green and
lemon, and she looked so much a part of the bright morning that Robin shot an examining look at herself. She
had simply tumbled in as she stood last night, only pulled
off her boots, and now her creased jodphurs, her
dishevelled shirt put her to shame.

Tamar Warren must have noticed, too, for he said laconically: 'Ragged Robin.'

As she stood a little sorry for herself, he added: 'Ablution block just through those few trees, Miss Mansfield.
You can bathe to your heart's content, there's a stream of
a sort, and I've scoured around for unwanted crawling
intruders and there aren't any.'

'Thanks.' She grabbed up a towel and some soap and
made for the trees.

There certainly was a stream in which to bathe, small,
yet flowing, and beneath it a natural saucer of rock in
which to sit. The first thing that Robin did was wash her
shirt, then hang it on a branch where the sun was shining. It was a seersucker and dried almost as she draped it
over.

The water was a boon. She soaped herself and let the
cool drip rinse away the suds. She put her hair under the

flow, let it stream through every strand, then she shook it out, combed it through and tied it back from her face with a narrow ribbon. Her shirt was dry now, and though her jodhpurs still looked slept-in she believed she looked fresher. Though never a Lilith in a yellow gown.

Ragged Robin. She heard him again and grimaced. She had never seen the English meadow flower; perhaps it was quite pretty, it must have been for her mother to have remembered it, but ragged she must appear and Robin she certainly was.

She went up to the fire where Noel and Lilith again were sharing the culinary chores.

'They look well, don't they?' It was Tamar walking by Robin's side. 'There's no greater encouragement to a man than to see a girl in an apron.'

'Lilith isn't wearing an apron.'

'I didn't mean that literally,' he said. 'I meant in spirit. There's no man born who doesn't like to think of a woman in a kitchen.'

'Including you?'

'I'm a man, too,' he pointed out mildly.

'And if a woman is not kitchen-inclined?'

'She can always change.' A pause. 'Or be changed.'

Robin tightened her lips. 'Well, one thing, you won't have to change Lilith.'

'I?' He turned round and looked at Robin.

'I forgot,' she came in blandly, 'you're the boss, the principal, never the teacher.'

'Perhaps I could be prevailed upon to give a lesson or two, though,' he submitted. He was still looking narrowly at her.

'But she doesn't need it,' said Robin. 'Lilith doesn't need it.'

'I didn't say Lilith.'

'But thought Lilith,' Robin said. Then she heard herself saying, and was shocked, yet somehow she could not

147

stop herself, 'Though how you could think like that is still beyond me, for obviously you adored your father.'

Tamar said: 'Yes, I did.'

'And yet you would – you intend to—'

'Yes?'

'You would—'

'Yes?'

'You know what I'm trying to say,' she endeavoured uncomfortably.

'As a matter of fact, Miss Mansfield, I have no idea.'

That 'Miss Mansfield' once more did it. It stiffened Robin's daring.

'Then' ... she drew a breath ... 'how could you like what your father liked?' she fairly burst out.

'To me it sounds both reasonable and desirable. My father had excellent taste.'

'But doesn't it seem ... well, doesn't it sound to you like it sounds to me? A kind of depriving him? A sort of robbing his memory? I mean—'

'Look, I just can't follow you. Not at all. Apparently you like to remember your grandfather, don't you?'

'That's different.'

'Because he was a Mansfield and my father was a Warren?'

'No' ... boldly ... 'because Lilith is a Warren, too,' Robin said pointedly. 'With – with you, she would be the second Mrs. Warren, wouldn't she?'

He looked at her a long enigmatical moment.

Then: 'Quite so,' he agreed at length. 'So what?'

'Doesn't it seem – in wrong taste to you?'

'Not at all.'

'Your father's wife? I mean, his wife before yours? I mean – when you two were so close?'

'But Lilith was not.'

'Not what?'

'My father's wife.'

'She married him,' Robin argued.

'She did not.'

'You said so . . . also Mathew was here because—'

'Yes, I said so . . . and Mathew came, and all Yarani "heard talk". But Lilith did *not* marry my father. Time – his time – didn't allow. I found that out when I went across.'

'I never knew,' whispered Robin.

He shrugged.

'But Lilith Warren?' she still disbelieved.

'She was previously a Mrs. Warren, it's not such an uncommon name after all.'

'Mathew John Warren,' Robin recalled a little stupidly, remembering Pablo's answer to her question. She realized now that the little boy had been speaking the truth.

So, she thought, there was nothing after all to keep Tamar from asking Lilith. There hadn't been all along, of course, not actually, but now – well, the situation was something more than actual, if things can be more than actual, it was – it was—

'Breakfast!' called Noel, and Lilith Warren, but not the Warren Robin had thought she was, called brightly: 'Will you make the tea, please, Tamar, you do it the best, and Robin, do come.'

Robin went over with her plate before she was told again, she did not want any unnecessary attention. She was glad that the fire could be blamed for any reddening of her cheeks, for she had been a fool, she knew.

She had been, and she borrowed from Tamar Warren, that female clot.

CHAPTER TEN

YET what else could she have thought? Robin brooded, eating, yet barely tasting Lilith's attractive breakfast, for either no one had considered the altered fact of Lilith's matrimonial state as needing discussion, or, and much more probable if the telling had been Tamar's prerogative, as Robin Mansfield as being entitled to be told.

No doubt, Robin's racing mind went on, if the omission had occurred to Tamar, he had dismissed it at once as nothing to do with her. Actually, Robin accepted unwillingly, that was so. Only, and she almost scalded her throat with a reckless gulp of boiling tea, what a difference the fact made. It established Pablo as not Tamar's stepbrother. It made Lilith not his dead father's wife.

But most of all, it laid a ghost.

Robin dwelt on that last in spite of herself, of her distaste. She thought of the loved ghost of Tamar's father who did not stand between Lilith and Tamar after all. For no one could have failed to recognize Tamar's deep affection for his father, and on her own recognition of it Robin had based an unadmitted yet innate certainty that in spite of Tamar's obvious attraction to the lovely Lilith he would never bring himself to—

'Robin, you're not eating.' It was Lilith and she was looking reproachfully across the camp fire. 'I have nothing to offer this expedition,' she regretted charmingly, 'except a hand with the cooking.'

'And what an achieving hand it is.' Tamar leaned over and touched the slender white fingers, such different fingers, Robin thought, from her own square brown ones, the ones Tamar once had advised her to attend to with polish and such, though little use, she shrugged, it would have been; she would never be a lily, only a ragged robin. Tamar was making no secret of his gesture. He even glanced up to see if Robin and Noel noticed.

They did.

A day's activities was being mapped out. But the time they left tomorrow, Tamar told Lilith, she should have a fair idea of this corner of Australia.

Corner! Lilith laughed, and indeed nothing could have been less like a corner, for the rise on which the men had rigged up the four one-man tents in which they had slept last night, had built the camp, looked endlessly out, or endlessly it seemed, on every side. Lilith having a small knowledge by this of the Yarani vista, Tamar intended now to give her a taste of its wider horizons.

'And I mean wider, Lilith,' he nodded, 'for from here, up or down, north or south, west ... but not east ... you're looking at the Inside, as we call it. You'll be struck by the different terrain, as my grandfather was struck. He knew then that he didn't have to stick at sheep.' He did not glance at Robin as he said it, but she did not need any look.

'Perhaps he would be sorry about that now,' she said.

He smiled as one does to a rather stupid child. 'The fleece is turning gold?' he taunted. 'Tell all your balls of wool, all of them, to say that to just one of my Brahma boys.'

'Your wool now,' she reminded him, and would have gone further had not Noel intervened with a disgusted:

'You two!'

How wrong Noel was, Robin thought. They were Tamar Warren and Robin Mansfield, and together they would never add up to two.

Tamar suggested spending the morning on the stones of the Palisades, and as soon as the meal was finished they began.

151

Unlike the Devil's Marbles, those gigantic granite boulders that were attracting tourists to the Northern Territory, the rocks here, though granite, too, and the same rich colour, were different in shape. Instead of round apples, plump cottage loaves, moulded spheres, the Palisades were serrated, and the outcrops took on amazing shapes of turrets, spires, terraces and bosses. Mostly they were red, but where shadows formed from a larger rock they turned blue or bruised violet.

'We named this one Split Rock,' remembered Robin excitedly from old days.

'You might have, but I called it the Bread Knife,' tossed Tamar from a balancing rock with a small abyss between it and the one Robin poised on.

Noel and Lilith had found a seesaw rock but had the good sense to try it out; it had stood like that for years, hundreds, thousands, perhaps millions of years, but, as Tamar called out this could be the year of change, who knew? Instead they looked out on a new country for Lilith, on a new terrain for Noel, looked out on skeleton weed, dried gullies and scalded flats on one side on the distant greening of Yarani on the other side.

They climbed down again and began examining the base of the Palisades. The rocks were a flaming gold and burning to touch where the sun hit them, but in the shadows the purple dimness was like entering a cool room.

Absorbed with the wonder of it, they met, divided up, met again. Robin was examining a small granite specimen not unlike a toadstool when she heard Lilith's little cry. It was not a frightened gasp, so she dismissed any further snake encounter, but she did make her way to where she believed the voice came. It could be one of those fantastic frilled lizards, or dragons, that frequented these rocks, that was absorbing Lilith, and though it was innocuous Lilith would be advised not to pick it up, both for herself since in fright the creature might inflict a bite, but also for the reptile, which was not intended for human handling.

But when she turned a corner she smiled with Lilith. How the dingo pup had got there they would never know, since the dingo was firmly controlled out here; the reward for the scalp of any that did get in was ten dollars.

But this little fellow obviously knew none of that, and, like all dingo puppies, he was outrageously attractive. He was saffron yellow and had matching white splashes on his feet and tail. His ears had pixie points.

'He's sweet,' said Lilith. 'Can we keep him?'

'No,' Tamar, who must have heard Lilith's cry as well, said firmly, and this time Robin agreed. Though she had two minds as to whether the dingo was all he was painted, and that was savage, mean, unreliable, she knew he was wild, and with dogs at every Yarani station you simply couldn't allow such a risk.

Lilith was sensible if regretful. They all agreed that as the pup was too young to leave they would make a journey out to an aboriginal camp some miles north and known to Tamar and Robin where the little fellow would be welcome.

'They're household pets there,' Tamar explained.

As they rode out, the dingo pup tucked under Tamar's arm, and apparently not at all upset by this method of distance covering, Robin and Tamar told the others of the Kedgee tribe.

The tribe was young in European years: Tamar said that his father, had he been alive, could have recalled that day when the Kedgees had appeared to drop out of the sky, men, women and children, the men and women in grass skirts, the children naked.

'Why did they come?' Lilith asked.

'Need,' said Tamar. 'There'd been a string of bad eating seasons. They knew of us if we didn't know of them, so they came in. They were duly fed, and, I'm sorry to say, clothed. But they had the good sense not to proceed any closer.'

'How close was that?'

'Where we're going now. It's where they stop. They know that in emergency we can help, but they prefer their own lives, which shows their wisdom. No petty arguments there, none, anyway, that can't be settled by the sharp end of a woomera instead of a tongue.'

'He's exaggerating, Lilith,' Robin came in, knowing that Tamar was referring to her, 'all that's in the dim ages now.'

'I still think it's a good settling method,' persisted Tamar, re-settling the pup in front of him and remarking feelingly as he did so that he always seemed to be carrying something lately, 'better, anyway, than words.' He glanced obliquely across at Robin.

On the outskirts of the camp they released the yellow pup.

'We won't go in,' Tamar said to Lilith, 'unless you particularly want to. I would have to seek out the Number One Man first and ask him, it's a courtesy they appreciate. Still, if you say—'

'I say I'd like that some other time, and with some toys and sweets,' said Lilith, for a shy little girl had run out to claim the yellow pup, and where children were, rewards should be, Lilith was obviously thinking.

'That will be done,' sealed Tamar. 'It's for you to say when.' Now it was Lilith he was looking at. It was no oblique glance as at Robin. It was a long seeking look.

Robin, watching the exchange, saw Lilith flush prettily as she turned her head away. Digging in her heels, Robin urged Ribbons on to where Noel now led the way back to the camp.

The manager had little to say today. He responded sparsely to Robin's determined chatter, he seemed depressed for Noel, for even when Tamar's second in command had related the story of his first tragic marriage there had been a sadness there, yet never a depression.

With a little sigh Robin gave up trying to force the conversation.

Some geologists in the distance poking around with the gear that had become as accepted in the Inside as the old prospector's dolly pot attracted the men's attention, and they decided to ride out. The girls declined to go, preferring to sit beneath one of the few trees that offered until they returned.

'What will it be?' Lilith asked with interest as Noel and Tamar rode off.

'They'll be looking for "signs",' Robin told her, 'nickel, though even when you find signs you carefully say "rocks." '

'Why?'

'Because the wind has ears.'

'Then those men won't welcome our boys out there?'

'They won't mind farmers, in fact they're anxious to be friendly with the farmer. At Nooroo, running sheep, there's no problem, but straying cattle could break legs in the holes the geos might leave behind, so naturally they're more congenial to a land man than an under-the-land type. By that I mean a prospector or a miner.'

'I can't think how they could ever find anything,' said Lilith, looking around her. 'It all seems the same to me.'

'To me, too, but if you carry a magnet, you would know it isn't. Mainly they look for outcrops where subterranean rocks have surfaced. Then if the outcrops have nickel you'll feel the pull of the magnet. If it is a big find, that's the start of the technocrats with their magnetometers, percussion drills and the rest.'

'You know a lot about it, Robin.'

'Through Jim, my twin, who was very interested in what happened under but never above the ground.'

'Yes, Tamar told me you were the farmer.'

'Born the wrong sex,' said Robin.

'Not really,' Lilith smiled. 'I believe you wouldn't

change the arrangement as it stands for the world.'

'Some think it would be better,' said Robin. She was thinking of Tamar and his advice of her hands, her nails, her lack of cookery skill – everything female, it had seemed.

'I'm sure they don't,' said Lilith.

A comfortable silence encompassed them. It was hot, but a pleasant golden heat, no enervation in it, just a drowsy desire to do nothing for a while.

All they did was watch the receding men, then as the figures grew less distinct and the sun danced on the plain, they both slept a little.

They woke together. In the distance they could see the figures becoming slowly but progressively larger. The men were coming back.

'Lilith,' Robin said a little abruptly, 'I thought you'd married Mr. Warren.'

'I did.'

'I mean – Tamar's father.'

'Yes, I suppose you would think that. It was all arranged – the date, the church. Then Laurence . . .' She gave a little sensitive lift of her slender shoulders.

'I'm sorry,' Robin said.

'Be more sorry for Tamar. He loved his father.'

'And you?'

'Laurence Warren was perhaps the finest man I've ever met. I would have married him, Robin, and made it a good marriage, only' . . . again the little lift . . . 'it was not to be.'

As Robin did not speak, Lilith resumed: 'If you can, think of it from my side. I'd been alone . . . oh, I had Mat, of course, but a child, however lovable, however loved, is still a child, is still no company, for many years. Also, I had a financial struggle, a struggle I knew would end with Laurence. He was lonely, too. His wife died when Tamar was born, but I suppose now you know all that.'

'Yes. What I did not know about was your non-mar-

156

Except, thought Robin with sudden fear, I hope it is only that, I hope it is only looking.

For this wurlie was not the usual mere cleft in a rock, it was far larger than that, it was large enough for someone to immerse themselves in, even swim a few strokes. And that, feared Robin, was what Lilith could have done. The fact that it was a drinking hole would not stop her, for on this expedition it was a hole for the horses only, except in emergency, and since Tamar had announced this, had said they would drink from their own supply from flasks and demijohns, Lilith would feel she was doing no wrong.

For herself, Robin would never have dreamed of cooling down in that deep hole, for she knew how cold, not just cold compared to the plain temperature but freezingly cold, those waters could be. But Lilith was a new-chum, she was a tired, hot, unaccustomed English girl, the water would have enticed, and she—

'Lilith!' Robin cried, and she began to run.

She knew vaguely she was covering distance in less time than she had ever covered it, even at school on a smooth green oval, parents cheering. And this was no smooth green. And no one cheered.

It was silent. There was no silence anywhere, Robin believed, like the silence here. The bush around Yarani was full of birds twittering, crickets whirring, but when the grass gave out and the red earth took over, the only noise was the quick scuttle of a lizard, the slither of other ground things, and they were so furtive they were barely ever heard. Grandfather had held her hand once, she remembered, and said: 'You are now in the silent world.'

She could believe it more than ever. Nothing seemed to stir ... especially that deep green surface of the water which she had reached by now, and was kneeling beside, staring down.

It was a surprisingly dark pool for an exceedingly light country, for out here the scientists had declared there was a brighter degree of light than anywhere else in the world. But then the wurlie was entirely rock-circled, almost tented, you could say, by jutting, overhanging stones.

Now Robin nearly touched the water with her eyes. Unlike other sheets of water, the water here did not weave beneath the surface, it was still, almost solidly still, almost like a giant block of ice.

And icy it would be, Robin knew, so icy that anyone jumping in from the heat outside would be so shocked that they—

It was then Robin saw it, that slender white arm. She did not wait to peer further, she dived deeply in at once.

But before she did so she remembered to open her mouth and shout out. One terrified, alerting, piercing scream.

Robin knew the numbing cold would soon take away any plan for action, so any action had to be now, not a moment's delay. It would need to be instant regardless of the cold, for she did not know how long that arm had been like that. Robin pushed down the moment the icy water took her to it, opened her eyes in the glass-like green, glimpsed flesh, grabbed, pulled.

Lilith, thank heaven, was not here. Between the rock clefts, trees sometimes sprang up, and a broken branch that had dropped in could have encircled the girl. There was one now touching Robin's leg. She kicked at it, then she kicked upward. Lilith came with her.

She shoved the girl's head above surface, afraid to look at her. Anyway, she had something more immediate to do, she had to push her out of the hole as soon as possible, the cold made that very important; if she stopped longer, if either of them stopped longer, it could be fatal, but how could she lever Lilith out? It seemed impossible.

She screamed again, but she felt it was a pitiful alarm. Lilith was a dead weight, and something seemed to be pulling Robin under again.

She kicked, and was released, but only temporarily. She felt her foot entangled once more. But she still held Lilith's face up.

'Help, someone!' It was only a croak, but Robin blessedly was not aware of that. When the men's steps resounded round the rocks as they encircled the hole, she believed that Tamar and Noel had heard her.

They had not. Faintly only they had heard that first scream, they had been some distance away then, but returning to the camp, finding the girls gone, they had recalled that cry, and come across.

Between them now they released Robin of her burden, and at once Noel was on his knees beside the girl affording resuscitation.

And at once, unseen at first in the men's concern for Lilith, Robin slipped back into the glassy depths.

It was not exhaustion, it was not the awful numbness she was suffering, it was the thing that had caught at her foot before. It would be an old log that had fallen in, become water-heavy and sunk to the bottom, but still retained its stripped branches, branches to reach up and entangle and entrap. It was entangling her now, but she had not the strength left this time to kick it off. I'm going to drown, Robin knew.

Then someone was pulling her, pushing her, shoving her, forcing back the thing that entangled her. She and Tamar were rising to the surface together.

He edged her out first, then slid out after her. For a while she just lay where he had pushed her, staring at a patch of blue sky between the rocks – *blue*, she knew with relief, not icy-green any more.

Then she saw Noel cradling Lilith. He had ceased his resuscitation because she had responded, and now he was simply holding the girl in his arms, and Lilith was quietly remaining there. But there was a tenderness as well as quiet, an infinite, unmistakable gentleness on both sides that sent Robin's eyes seeking Tamar's.

'Poor you,' she said impulsively, and turned her own glance sympathetically away.

Noel carried Lilith out of the rock enclosure into the sunshine, into the warmth that would bring the circulation back to her numbed limbs. Robin and Tamar were left by the wurlie's edge.

Suddenly Robin was aware of Tamar Warren looking incredulously at her, looking angrily.

'You fool,' he told her, 'you utter little fool!'

'Before you said clot,' she reminded him weakly.

'Be quiet! Be quiet, anyway, if all you can say is a fool thing like that, like "Poor you." Good lord, you didn't think . . . you couldn't think . . .'

'I thought,' Robin answered. 'I still do.'

'Then think this.' Without any warning his lips crushed down on hers.

She still couldn't believe it. Robin was thinking this as she and Lilith bounced along in the Glenville jeep over the unmade track to Nooroo.

They had not stopped at the Palisades after the wurlie incident. They had broken camp as soon as Lilith was fit, then ridden as far as a jeep could be brought from Yarani. Tamar had gone ahead, then later come back behind a waggon and driver, then, after putting the two girls in the back seat, he and Noel had set off the same way as they had come, on horseback, but this time towing the surplus horses.

Lilith, still exhausted, had closed her eyes as soon as they had started off, and in a short time had slept. Just as well, Robin had thought, for the driver had to pick his way and at times the going was over a patch of gibber. She looked at the girl's head that had slipped on to her shoulder. She had been very brave, Robin thought, after the ordeal was over she had helped break camp like the rest of them. She would make a fine country wife . . . for

Noel. That seemed a dream, but it wasn't, it was true, and in the short time they had together as they had stowed their things back in their packs, Lilith had said so.

'I suppose you're surprised, Robin.'

'Yes, you two certainly never looked like—'

'The moment I saw Noel, I knew. I knew why he was so important to Mathew, I knew because in that minute of first seeing him he was important, too, to me.'

'I thought it was you – and Tamar.'

'I suspected that. But I could scarcely say "It's Noel" when I didn't know how Noel felt.'

'He seemed to avoid you, and you certainly avoided him.'

'Sometimes things are so – so unbelievable you are afraid to come nearer to them for fear they dissolve. Can you understand that?'

'Yes,' nodded Robin. Presently she said: 'You know, Lilith, I believe Noel loved you even before he met you. He used to talk of you as Mathew's mother just as though he was Mathew's father himself.'

'He will be,' Lilith smiled. 'I think Tamar had that in mind right from the beginning. He's an old friend of Noel's, and the death of Noel's young wife was a sorrow to him as well.'

'Yes, he even considered me as a possible solace,' nodded Robin, 'or so Noel once said.'

'Then Noel was not perceptive, it was never you. You were for Tamar – I could see that at once.'

'Then I couldn't,' said Robin. 'I'm not sure if I can now.' But she said it happily. She *felt* sure. There had been no more words yet, there had been no time, but the memory of those eyes coming closer to her eyes, that intense 'Then think this,' the lips on hers . . . Yes, she was sure.

When they reached Nooroo, between them Mrs. Mac and Robin put Lilith to bed. Mrs. Mac brought in warm milk, pulled down the blind, then the housekeeper nodded for Robin to follow her to the kitchen.

'She'll be all right,' the motherly woman said, 'but I wanted to see to her first before I saw to you.'

'I'm all right, Mrs. MacPherson.'

'But right enough to keep travelling?'

'What do you mean?' Robin stared at Mrs. MacPherson. 'Is anything wrong? My mother? Ginny? Jim?'

'No, dear, but your brother has phoned twice today asking for you.'

'What did he say?'

'That he wants you down there as soon as you can go,' the woman told her.

'Did he say why?'

'He seemed to think you would know yourself.'

—Yes, thought Robin dully, he would think I knew. — And I do. For it was the break, the break she had seen coming. But what did Jim think *she* could do?

'I won't go,' she said.

'He sounded very anxious.'

'I'm not anxious.' Only anxious to stop here, Robin thought, hear the rest of what Tamar has to say.

'At least ring him,' Mrs. MacPherson urged gently.

'With Lilith just slipping off to sleep?'

'Go over to Glenville and ring there. Mathew went across, anyway, so he has to come back.'

'Well, I could fetch him, I suppose,' Robin agreed unwillingly. She did not say whether she would phone.

But when she got to the big homestead she went to the study where she would be private. It took a while to get through, then she was hearing Jim's voice.

'Oh, thank heaven, Robbie! When are you leaving?'

'I'm not.'

'You're needed, Rob, I can't send down for Mother.'

'I should think not, Jim, but I still—'

'Robbie, come!' he begged.

'I've something important here.'

'Not as important as this. Look, I'm expecting you on

164

tomorrow's train. I'll be there at Central. Leave it at that.'

'Jim—'

But his phone had gone down.

Important. How important was holding a marriage together between two people who, if they had cared enough, would have held it together themselves? Was it as important as – as something still unsaid but the words waiting there?

'Ragsy, I need you to do up these buttons.'

Pablo always had trouble with buttons, so Robin went out mechanically to the little boy to help him.

Then she paused. I need you, Pablo had said, and so had Jim. I need you. Her twin had needed her. She must go after all. The other could – and would – wait.

'Mrs. Mac will do it for you when Tamar drives you home, darling,' she said. She added: 'Or Mummy if she's awake.'

'Why aren't you driving me home?'

'Because I'm not going home. I'm going to Sydney. It's important.'

'Are you going right down in the car?'

'Only as far as the train.' Robin had glanced at her watch and had seen she could catch the evening mail if she hurried. 'You can tell one of the men to pick the car up at the station.'

'And what do I tell Tamar?' Mathew asked.

That I love him? thought Robin. No . . . I have to say that myself.

'That I've gone,' she answered instead.

In half an hour she was on the Sydney train.

CHAPTER ELEVEN

THE train in the old days when Robin had travelled back to her Sydney school from Yarani had always gone too quickly, and even young as she had been she had known it was because she had left her heart behind. How, she had asked an indifferent twin travelling back to his school, can you live without a heart?

Jim, unimpressed, had said she would pick it up on the next vacation.

But this time, Robin thought, gazing out of the window, it was different, for even though she was leaving Yarani, she still felt the train was dawdling, and she wanted it to hurry, *hurry*, so she could get this Sydney bit over. Get back to Tamar.

She knew Tamar would be angry when he returned and found she had gone. Between them as the jeep with the girls and the horses with the men had parted had stretched something sweet and surprised but as yet unsaid. Only those few words had been said. 'Then think this.' Then there had been Tamar's lips on hers.

The rest would have come tonight, Robin had known that, and every minute since it had happened she had waited in a sort of blurred rosiness. Now she would have longer to wait, she thought, and so would Tamar.

Tamar and Robin. It was still unbelievable. Never for a moment had she dreamed that Tamar had felt like that. For one thing there had been Lilith. But now ... still incredulous ... it was Noel and Lilith, leaving—

Oh, it's too wonderful, Robin thought, it's too – too—

When had she first loved him? Robin knew it had started as far back as a little boy coming with his stepbrother, or stepbrother Robin had thought, and peeping under Ribbons at her and asking: 'Are you English, then?' She remembered feeling angry at the man for blowing the horn for the child to run back to him ... but even then, and that far between them, she had felt an unwilling, unadmitted attraction. Unwilling because he was a Glenville even though his name was Warren, unadmitted because even to herself Robin had not dared believe it. Because of her unbelief she had fought him, but it had only taken three words, 'Then think this' to break down her wall.

She had been too late to get a sleeper, but Robin was used to sitting up in a train. When she had had to take a job in the city, travelling second sitting had been her only hope of coming home. – A job in the city. That seemed another life now.

She shut her eyes and resigned herself to the rhythmical roll of the wheels. It was almost dark, a time she always loved in trains.

The job in the city brought Ginny to her mind, for every day after work she had returned to Ginny's apartment. If she had never gone there in the first place Ginny and Jim never might have met. Never have married.

And now it was all over. Jim's voice over the phone had been a worried one. He wanted his twin with him, though whether it was to bolster him up or to plead with Ginny, Robin could not think. On the other hand it might have been Jim who had made the break. All Robin was really sure of was that the two of them never had been happy at Nooroo. She had hoped they might settle whatever differences they had away from the country, but now she knew that they had not.

Then I, frowned Robin next, I left no message for Tamar. But what could I have written?

'I've gone to Sydney because my brother and sister-in-law no longer love each other.'

No, she could not have put what had happened to those two in words, not in her very first letter. It would have to wait, and ... Robin repeated that thought ... Tamar would be angry.

He could always expect things to be done the correct way, he would be self-disciplined, autocratic, he would demand as good as he gave, and he would never, Robin knew, leave, as she had left, without a word.

But, the rhythm of the train beginning to put weights on her eyelids now, what did it matter? They loved each other, and that would be her message ... and Tamar's reply.

Robin slept and awakened as train travellers do throughout the night. People got in at country stations, people got out. Around piccaninny daylight, Robin climbed rather giddily from her carriage and took scalding tea at a tiny station bar, for remote Yarani was not serviced by a diner as were most New South Wales trains, travelling was still the same as years ago.

But, eating a varnished station bun, swallowing brown liquid from an enamel cup, she knew she liked it this way. She went back, then as a first ray of sunlight buttered the sill of her window seat, she went and washed in the small ablutions compartment.

She looked at herself in the speckled mirror, wondering if she had outwardly changed from the girl who had train-travelled like this only six months ago, because it was six months since Ginny and Jim had married and made these snatched journeys home no longer necessary.

Six months, yet now Ginny and Jim ...

Robin looked away from the speckled mirror, feeling anxious again.

Her anxiety when the train pulled in at Sydney Central and Jim came up to help her with her bag. Always grave, Jim now looked a monument of concern.

In the car Robin touched his hand briefly; they had never been demonstrative, but each had appreciated that understanding touch.

'Robby.' Jim actually raised a smile.

'How is Ginny?'

'Well, she's being very resolved about it.'

'And you?'

'I'm worried to hell, you know me.'

'Yes, I know you, darling, always Atlas holding up the world.'

'But with you here, Robby – well—' He gave another determined grin and shrugged.

'I won't be able to do much.'

'You'll be *here*,' Jim emphasized.

'But not long.' – Oh, Jim, Robin wanted to cry out, I love you, and I'd like to stay and help you, but can't you see a change in me, can't you see I've fallen in love?

'You've not changed.' That seemed funny to Robin after what she had just cried out about herself. 'I suppose it's because it's still Yarani as ever.'

'I suppose so.'

'And Tamar?' Jim looked searchingly at her. 'Oh, I know it wasn't anything at first, not really, I know it was all a ruse, but now?'

'Now it's Tamar,' Robin said, and her eyes shone.

Jim nodded and touched her hand in his turn. Then he appealed: 'But you'll see us out of this spot, Rob?'

'I don't know why I'm needed, but yes, I will.'

'Thank you. As for the need – well, you may not be as domesticated as some' . . . he grinned all the way now . . . 'but you'll fit the bill.'

Robin did not quite follow that, and said so. 'You mean a shoulder to lean on?' she asked. 'Female sympathy?'

'If female sympathy includes a cup of tea now and then and being there, yes.'

'Rob, what on earth are you talking about?'

'Well, *I* can't give it to Ginny, not during the day. Naturally, *and now especially,* I have to be at work. Then no hospital will accept a patient just for lying-in, not these overcrowded days.' As Robin still stared at him, Jim concluded: 'And it has to be, Doctor Cooper says it's a very crucial time.'

There was a silence as Jim negotiated a snarl in the city traffic.

'Say that again,' said Robin. 'No – no, don't. Say it in simple words, Jim.'

'Say what?'

'That patient bit to begin with. What patient?'

'Ginny, of course. Though, as Doctor Cooper says, a patient is what she must not think herself.'

'Who?'

'Ginny.'

'... Ginny?' she echoed.

'Well' ... humorously ... 'it's not me.'

'Ginny is ill?'

'*Not* ill. That's another thing Doctor Cooper says.'

'Then – then what's the matter with her, Jim?'

Her brother looked at Robin quickly and incredulously, it had to be a quick look in this city traffic.

'She's a mother-to-be, you idiot!'

'Clot,' Robin said mechanically. 'You mean you ... you mean Ginny ...'

'I mean both of us. It's generally like that. Good heavens, Robby, why the surprise? It does happen.'

'But I thought it was—'

'Yes?'

'I thought of something else,' Robin said lamely. Oh, Tamar, she was thinking, I *could* have left a note after all, I could have written:

'I'm helping Ginny and Jim whose love has flowered.' Then, she smiled to herself, I could have finished:

'I send my love.'

She looked at her twin and grinned. Jim grinned back.

'But, Rob, I told you!' Ginny, sitting up in bed and wearing a negligée that must have cost her adoring husband

... yes, adoring, accepted Robin ... more than his week's salary, and he had assured his twin that it was a very good one, thanks to Tamar, looked at Robin incredulously.

'It was Jim who first started me on that train of thought,' Robin shrugged, 'though I did have qualms over you two at Nooroo.'

'Our incompatibility with the land, though never with each other, must have shown.'

'It did.'

'Then try not to blame us for it. I'm sorry, Rob, if you can't see it our way, or perhaps I should say if we can't see it yours. You're born for the country, or you're not, it's as simple as that. We were not. We would have stuck it out if we had to, but we didn't have to, thank goodness. Don't think badly of us because we escaped.'

'I'm just thinking incredulously of you.'

'Of two happily married people.'

'Yes, you are, aren't you? But I didn't think ... I feared ...'

'It hadn't worked? Robin, you must know your brother, always a sobersides. Then I don't exactly bubble. I'm the quiet sort. But it's there, our love for each other, even though you didn't see it. Our apparent unhappiness was our mutual dislike of what fate had dished us up, yet you thought—'

'I also thought it when I got Jim's letter in answer to mine telling him I might soon be down. He replied "... about seeing you soon, Rob, that will be good, though not, I'm afraid under this roof."'

'I'll have a word with him, we can always find room for you, Robbie.' Ginny leaned over and took Robin's hand. Presently she said 'And you took that as—'

'As the beginning of the split between you. Then when I rang you—'

'I told you.'

'Yes,' nodded Robin, 'and it was a bad connection and I never heard.'

'That was why you said "Be sure",' recalled Ginny. 'I took it as being sure over our news,' she laughed.

Robin laughed with her. Everything was just too wonderful, she thought, touching the wood of her arm-rest, for touching wood had been her good luck omen as a child. Ginny and Jim are rapturously happy.

As I intend to be.

During the three weeks that followed ... it was a crucial period in Ginny's pregnancy and she had to be kept in bed, though no busy city hospital would find room for such an obviously well young woman ... Robin took out pen and paper a dozen times.

But what to say?

Besides ... a little pique slipping in, but a delicious expectant pique ... Tamar, too, could have written.

In the end, Robin did not communicate Tamar did not communicate. But it did not matter, Robin smiled often to herself, Tamar had looked into her eyes and said: 'Then think this' before his lips had met hers. It was more exciting this way, she wanted to *hear*, not read, the sweetness. It would be all the lovelier when it happened.

She put aside her impatience for Tamar and actually enjoyed the waiting — rather like a bud must, she thought whimsically, when it is waiting to bloom.

'You're the most patient of nurses,' commended Ginny.

'You're the most compliant mother-to-be,' smiled Robin.

'It's worth it. This is our first harvesting, Rob, and we both want it to go through beautifully.'

'It will.'

'Thanks to you, darling. — Oh, Doctor Cooper said I can live a normal life by the end of the week.'

'That means I can go home.' Robin was not aware she said it so eagerly.

'Has it been that bad?' Ginny laughed.

'Of course not. I've enjoyed it Only—'

'I know.' A pause from Ginny. 'I think I knew all along.'

'What, Ginny?'

'Well, you and Tamar did announce an engagement, remember.'

'It was only a cover then.'

'I knew that, too, yet I knew at the same time that it was a beginning. *The* beginning. There's a look, Robbie, a certain look. You two had it.'

'We didn't know then, or at least I didn't. Well, anyway, I wasn't aware of it if I did.'

'No, sometimes you're not.'

'Were you aware with Jim?'

'From the moment I met him.'

'And yet – well, there was another, Ginny.'

'Oh, that!' Ginny laughed, and shrugged.

The rest of the week went just as pleasantly. Now that the end was in sight Robin found herself just as anxious to eke out the moments as she was anxious for the moments to fly. She knew she was a little nervous at meeting Tamar again, but a delicious nervousness, a shyness she had never known she possessed.

Then the last day arrived, and Ginny, up and coping, hugged her sister-in-law.

'Thank you for little Jim's sake,' she smiled.

'Or small Ginny's?'

'It's a boy. But thank you, anyway. And Rob—'

'Yes?'

'Don't let it go on and on like it did with me.'

'With—?'

'With Tamar and me.'

'Tamar?' echoed Robin.

'Of course. But you knew.' Ginny was moving around the room, so she did not see Robin's suddenly ashy face. 'After all, Tamar Warren is scarcely a common name,' she laughed.

No, but you never told me it was Tamar Warren,

Robin was saying, but in her incredulity not saying it aloud.

'Even if you hadn't heard me,' Ginny was continuing, 'you must have noticed the way Tamar spoke to me as Ginny at once.'

'Yes.' This time Robin did speak aloud.

'Jim has the car out to take you to the station. Thanks again.' Now Ginny crossed and kissed her. 'You're a little pale,' she said. 'We've worked you too hard, Tamar will be angry, he'll have something to say.'

Tamar had everything to say, but Robin doubted if she would listen. She doubted if she would say anything ... ever ... to him.

The train back was going far too fast, the train that Robin Mansfield, schoolgirl, had urged impatiently on and on. Now she wished it would never get there.

'Don't let it go on and on like it did with me ... with Tamar and me.' Robin heard that with every turn of the wheels. She had been a fool not to have guessed; on Tamar's own words he had been away for years studying Promotion, and that man ... Ginny had been wrong there, she had never said his name ... had been away, too. The States, Robin thought.

Ginny had seemed untouched by it all, but undoubtedly the eagerness and surety of her husband had done that. – But what about Tamar?

It was all foolish, her common sense told Robin that, it had all happened before she had known Tamar. But did she want to know him better, as these last delirious weeks had made her believe she did, any more?

Besides ... and there was a finger of hurt on Robin's heart ... I didn't want to come *after* someone else. I wanted the spring. The greening. This is a second season, she knew.

She did not rest. This time she had purchased a sleeper, but she spent the night at the window, staring out. Staring at things flashing past. That was wrong, they themselves were flashing, but it didn't matter, for she didn't see them, anyway. Her eyes were blurred with tears.

She had never known love before ... except her love for Nooroo. At the age when most girls are meeting it, she had remained the same rather odd ... she supposed odd ... Nooroo-obsessed little country girl.

But now the land she loved would never be hers. She could not stay at Yarani any more.

By morning Robin knew she wasn't functioning properly any more; she hadn't eaten, hadn't slept, her head was whirling round.

When the train pulled in at the small station she was tempted not to jump off, to go on. But the next stop was some twenty miles further, and it would mean that someone would have to come and get her, for, even though she did not intend to stay, first there were things that had to be done.

When she stepped on to the small platform, all the train as usual peering through the window to see why they had stopped at such a small place, who was getting off, Robin's legs were buckling under her.

'You all right?' asked Wattie, concerned. 'You look all in, Miss Robin.'

'I'm all right.' I'm all right except tired, knew Robin, and so long as *he* isn't here I'll get by.

'Boss is away,' Wattie went on.

Yes, that would be typical, Robin thought perversely now, forgetting it was what she wanted, that was how it went with Ginny. He was never there.

'Won't be back till the end of next week,' resumed Wattie.

Now Robin mentally registered: 'I'll be left by then. I'll even be gone by tomorrow.'

But at Nooroo Lilith had different ideas, and though Robin held out, refused, shook her head, when Noel added his pleas, then Mathew, she had to give in.

175

For Lilith and Noel were being married.

'Mrs. Mac could look after Mat, we know that, and he likes her very much, but you, Robin—'

'But you're my own sister, Ragsy,' Mathew finished.

'I don't know,' Robin tried to escape. 'You see, Ginny needs me.'

'Oh, Rob' ... it was Lilith ... 'Ginny rang. She must have thought you got in earlier than you did. Something she said she forgot to say to you. She wants to tell you now.'

She said everything, Robin knew.

'Will you, Robin?' Lilith asked.

'Will you, old girl?' Noel.

'Ragsy?' begged Pablo.

'Yes,' Robin said to Mathew ... so said to them all.

Robin had thought that Lilith and Noel would have wanted to wait for Tamar's return for the ceremony; after all, the union to be was really his doing. He had wanted his friend married ... even had had ideas about Robin herself for the manager at one time, though Lilith had shook her head at that. She had acclaimed that Tamar had had something else in view. – A long view, Robin thought, how many years had Ginny waited?

'All Tamar wants is for us both to be together,' Lilith smiled, 'the last thing he said when I rang him—'

'You rang him?'

'Yes, he's cattle buying up at Rochester. Tamar said: "The words don't matter, just so long as you two get the thing done." ' Lilith laughed. 'It's Yarani's turn for the circuit minister next week-end, so we thought we'd take the opportunity. He won't be around for another month.'

'And after the service?' Robin asked.

'Just a couple of days to ourselves before we become that little family that Mathew longs for,' appealed Lilith, and Robin noticed the pretty pink in her cheeks. She added, 'Please, Robin,' and Robin knew she could not refuse. But she did check on Tamar's return.

'He'll be away another week,' Lilith informed her. 'Noel says cattle-buying is demanding.'

'I wouldn't know, I only know sheep.' Robin turned away rather abruptly. She knew that Lilith's puzzled eyes were on her, but all Lilith said was: 'Don't forget that Ginny wants you to ring.'

Robin conveniently forgot. She was anxious to know how her sister-in-law was feeling, but if anything went wrong, if she was needed, she knew Jim would get in touch. This would be just a social call, and Robin felt at this juncture that she could not chatter with Ginny.

The wedding was a charming one, and much bigger than if the couple had waited for a city ceremony. Because if its isolation anything out of the daily run was a magnet out here, and literally everybody came, some leaving early in the morning and crossing miles of country to see the two wed. Because of this everyone was invited. Robin explained that to Lilith and the bride was delighted.

'I think it's lovely. They'll all come, too, to your wedding.'

My wedding? thought Robin.

At the last moment Robin was prevailed upon by Lilith to attend the bride. Knowing by this that Lilith was shrewd as well as lovely, Robin had no doubt that Lilith had left it to the last moment so as Robin could not refuse. Her timing with her: 'Robin, Noel says I simply have to have somebody by me and in the excitement I completely forgot. Will you—' did not deceive her.

'I'll have Mathew to watch,' she tried to evade.

'You won't be watching him, though, Mat is attending Noel.'

'I—'

'There'll be a bouquet to hand over when we exchange rings. I must have someone. Please, Rob!'

Once again Robin weakened.

She did add that she was going to look rather awful in

177

her old blue beside Lilith's buttercup silk.

'It's not old. It's still blue, though.' Lilith went to her wardrobe and brought out a dress that made Robin's eyes sparkle.

'You wretch,' she accused the bride fondly, 'you planned all this.'

'You have to plan a dress, otherwise—'

'You know what I mean. But oh, Lilith, it's lovely!'

'And it will fit, I can vouch for that. In lots of cunning ways I've been measuring you up all the week.'

Robin accepted that. She had tried on endless patterns, brown paper ones. She had thought that Lilith was cutting them out for herself and using Robin as the first fitting.

'Try it on,' Lilith urged.

Robin did, and it was a perfect fit.

The wedding morning had dawned bright and sunny with the promise of a bright and sunny afternoon. The ceremony had to be in the afternoon to give the further-outs a chance to get in. By four o'clock it had been decided that everyone would be in, so at four Lilith, with Robin behind her, met Noel, with Mathew behind him.

'Dearly beloved . . .' The church was small and brown, but its narrow windows looked out on a large brown landscape. Because garden flowers were hard to come by at Yarani, the ladies of the church had bundled any field ones they could. Salvation Jane, the farmer's curse, was a pretty curse nonetheless. There were some bowls of waterlilies, probably plucked at the peril of falling in as you did so, for if they were anything like Nooroo lilies, Robin recalled, the pads always opened up right in the middle.

' . . . we are gathered together . . .'

Robin looked at the gathering, the Garsides, the Gillespies who still had not left, the Frenshams—

And Tamar Warren.

He stood behind the back row and he looked across the

pews at Robin. She turned her glance the other way.

After the rings, the confetti, the signing, Lilith said: 'Wasn't it wonderful that Tamar got back in time?'

'Yes . . . because now I can return to Ginny.'

'Oh, yes, Rob' . . . abstractedly . . . 'did you ring Ginny?'

'And Mathew can be looked after by—' Robin stopped. No one was listening to her.

There was no worrying about any extra guest, always at any function out here the visitor brought a plate. There was insufficient room in the little Sunday School hall, but no one wanted to be inside, anyway, when there were trees to sit under outdoors.

Robin did not sit, she passed around frantically. She had a fear that if she stopped, Tamar would come across and say something, and she wanted to be very cool and to the point when she answered back.

It was rather a deflation, though, when he avoided her as much as she did him.

But at last the newlyweds were being waved away by the guests.

'It's a honeymoon,' explained Mathew to Robin. 'Before you start being a family you have to have one.'

'I see,' nodded Robin. 'Will we go home now?'

'Yes. Tamar is waiting in the car for us.'

He would, Robin thought. She had hoped he would return to Glenville with the boys, leave her and Pablo to find their own way.

But when they reached the car she was greeted airily and rather disinterestedly.

'Nice affair,' praised Tamar. 'You sitting by me, Mathew?' He released the brake and they drove off.

He even let them out at Nooroo without starting anything. 'I won't come in,' he informed them, 'I've had quite a day. 'Bye, Mat. Mum and Dad won't be long away.'

'Then it will be the family,' anticipated Mathew.

'Yes, sonno,' Tamar smiled. But he did not smile at Robin.

Robin and Mrs. MacPherson spent the next morning in characteristic female fashion. They discussed every dress of the women guests.

'Why do ladies like talking about dresses, Ragsy?' asked Mathew, who had come for a piece of Mrs. MacPherson's Cut and Come Again.

It was only when Tamar's drawling voice said: 'Silk, satin, cotton, rag, women are always interested, Mat,' that Robin knew he had come behind the boy.

'Rag,' nodded Mathew. 'But our Robin didn't wear it, though, she wore pebbles.'

'Polka dots,' said Robin, not looking up at Tamar.

'I came across,' said Tamar, 'to deliver several messages. It seems people have been ringing here, but no one has answered.'

Both Mrs. MacPherson and Mathew said they had been out for a while, Mathew having taken Mrs. MacPherson on a tour of Nooroo. The oldest and the youngest were now firm friends.

Robin said nothing. She had heard the several rings but not answered. She had only thought of Ginny calling, and she had shrunk, still, from speaking with Ginny.

'One ring was from your mum,' said Tamar to Mathew. 'She's having a fine time and will be home on Friday.'

Mrs. MacPherson, always ready with refreshment, had put a cup of tea down for Tamar.

'The other call,' said Tamar coolly, 'was from Sydney, from your brother's wife.' He looked curiously at Robin.

'Oh, yes.'

'You're to ring back.'

Robin nodded, but did not move. She still kept her eyes down.

When at length she looked up – after all, she could not sit like this indefinitely – Mrs. MacPherson and Mathew had left.

'I told them to,' Tamar nodded from across the table. 'And now I'm telling you to ring up Ginny.'

'In my own good time.'

'In my time. After all, this is my house.'

'I'm well aware of that, you never miss an opportunity to tell me. However, I can please myself when, or if, I ring.'

'When you ring will be now, as I might need the connection myself later. We're expecting a rather difficult birth, and Edwards will let me know the result.'

'That's when,' she said impertinently. 'I also said if.'

He answered: 'But I did not.'

'I hardly think that makes a difference.'

'Like what I said to you out at the Palisades made no difference either?'

'I don't know what you're talking about.'

'You do, but I'm the one who doesn't understand. You go away without a word.'

'I had to. Jim rang.'

'Without a word,' he continued, 'and stay away a month without a word.'

'It was three weeks,' she corrected.

'So you know that much,' he said, narrowing his eyes at her.

'Also you sent no word.'

'Every day I was expecting you. The days grew,' he shrugged.

'I could say the same.'

'Then say it. *Say it*, Robin.'

'No. Not now. I mean—'

'What do you mean?'

She did not answer.

'What do you mean?' His voice had not risen, but its question had. 'Explain yourself.'

'Ginny,' Robin said.

As he sat looking at her, she told him: 'The funny thing was that although I knew you'd been away, as he had, and had studied promotion, as he had, I never thought of you as him.'

'Whom are you talking about?'

'You, of course. Ginny's friend who kept her waiting all those years.'

'This is interesting. Please go on.'

'There's nothing to continue. It just stopped at that.'

'This is Ginny's story?'

'No ... well, yes, she did give me the outline, but the rest of it's my own version. You see, I was rooming with Ginny when the final curtain came down. I was there that night when Ginny came home.'

'You mean to tell me that all along you haven't known it was I who had—'

'I didn't know. I was stupid as usual.'

'A clot,' he agreed, but with no laughter now.

'Ginny called out to me just as I left for Yarani again, she said – "Don't let it go on and on like it did with me ... with Tamar and me." '

'And from that point you went on yourself?'

'Yes,' she said, and left it at that.

'You would never have brought yourself to ask her?'

'Would *you* bring yourself to ask?'

'I would. I'm going to now.'

He rose. Robin rose with him.

'No,' she said in distress.

'Why not?' he demanded. 'Why should I not ask Ginny what all this is about?'

'Because she's been ringing me and I haven't rung her back.'

'You didn't want to find out?'

'I didn't want to find out what I knew must be true.'

'That I kept this girl waiting while I made up my mind all those years?' he pressed.

'Yes,' Robin said defiantly.

'That now I was beginning to repeat my performance with you?'

'I ...'

But he did not wait for Robin to find words, he took her by the shoulders and impelled her to the telephone in the hall.

'Everyone will hear,' she cried. 'At least eight party liners will.'

'I don't care if all the world hears,' he replied, and picked up the receiver.

Leaning over him, Robin removed it and put it back in its cradle again.

'No,' she repeated.

'Because you don't want them to hear?'

'Not for that reason.'

'Because you want my explanation first?'

'Not for that, either.'

'Then?'

'Because – because I just don't believe it, Tamar.' Robin said it in a muffled voice, muffled because by the time she had reached his name her head was buried in his shoulder.

'Robin, Ragged Robin,' he was saying.

'I saw them, you know, sweetheart' ... sweetheart? ... 'it was the first thing I looked for in England.'

'What, Tamar?' she asked.

'Ragged Robin. Did you know you favoured wet marshy meadows, you little pink flower, so what are you doing in this brown land?'

'Tell me about Ginny,' Robin said; she felt she could not bear sweetness just now, not this much sweetness.

He shrugged whimsically. 'Believe it or not, it was Ginny who kept me dangling, she would never say Yes. For a simple reason, really, though I don't believe either of us ever recognized it. She didn't love me. I didn't love her. If we had been together continuously we would have reached that conclusion years before. But we were apart, and each time we came together again there was a newness, and a charm. But a charm only. A happy pleasant thing. We drifted into something we didn't really want, and when Ginny said what she did that last night, it was an immense relief. You see, I was wanting to say it, but how do you say such things to lovely girls? Anyway, she edged around it, and all at once we were laughing at each other.'

'She wasn't laughing when she came home.'

'She wasn't crying either, was she?' Tamar said. 'I think she was bemused, as I was, wondering how it had all begun.' He looked hard at Robin. 'I'm not asking you to believe this, I'm asking you to ask Ginny.'

'Perhaps I will . . . one day.'

'Do I have to wait till then?'

'Well, I'm waiting for you to finish what you said at the Palisades,' Robin answered. 'Be fair, Tamar.'

'Fair!' He laughed at her word. 'I could never be that with you. Don't you realize, you little idiot—'

'Clot.'

'That I loved you from that minute I saw you talking with a little boy in his own language, something I had failed to do.'

'Mathew is a funny little boy. I wouldn't judge your capacity to communicate with a child on young Pablo.'

'I'm not,' he said firmly. 'I intend to try on someone much more belonging.' His eyes held Robin's.

'You matched me with Noel.'

'Did you believe that?'

'No, but Noel—'

'Even that far back,' Tamar said, 'I had it all worked out. I knew it in detail after I returned from England. It was to be Noel and Lilith.   '

'I believed Lilith had married your father.'

'I'd thought so, too.'

'Then forgot to tell me when she hadn't'.

'So that when you learned the truth, you immediately set aside any feeling I might have had about not marrying Lilith myself.'

'Yes,' Robin said.

'You walk a devious path, young Robin,' he told her. 'I knew my direction all along.'

She did not answer that.

'You missed the right turns, you – What in heaven is that?'

For there was a noise that could only be horses galloping, yet Tamar had come across by car, and Ribbons was stabled. The fillies were still in the far northern paddock, Nightcap in the next field.

They looked at each other, then went out to the verandah.

Mathew and Mrs. MacPherson were there already, but so filled with wonder that neither were speaking, even Pablo stood in silence.

Cantering up the peppercorn drive to the homestead was Chief, big lovely wild Chief, but most amazing of all, and Tamar said it softly by Robin's side, was a young silver filly who rode with him.

'I've never seen it happen before,' Tamar said. 'He's brought her in, Robin.'

'And he's come back,' Robin nodded.

'As you have, Ragsy?' For a moment the big man turned his glance from the pretty scene to the girl.

'I never went, so I can't come back, can I?'

'You mean you're stopping here?'

'Right here, Tamar.'

'But not for long, *Mrs. Warren*,' he grinned. 'I don't know what your grandfather will do, for that matter I don't know what mine will, but the Glenvilles and the Mansfields are marrying and the two homesteads are knocking down a fence and becoming one.'

'Your Brahmas won't like that.'

'Neither will your balls of wool. But' . . . and the cattle-man drew her into his arms, 'I'll like it, Ragsy.'

That was when Robin said, as she used to as a child: 'Me, too.'

OMNIBUS — The 3 in 1 HARLEQUIN
only $1.50 per volume

Here is a great new exciting idea from Harlequin. THREE GREAT ROMANCES — complete and unabridged — BY THE SAME AUTHOR — in one deluxe paperback volume — for the unbelievably low price of only $1.50 per volume.

We have chosen some of the finest works of four world-famous authors . . .

VIOLET WINSPEAR

ISOBEL CHACE

JOYCE DINGWELL

SUSAN BARRIE

. . . and reprinted them in the 3 in 1 Omnibus. Almost 600 pages of pure entertainment for just $1.50 each. A TRULY "JUMBO" READ!

These four Harlequin Omnibus volumes are now available. The following pages list the exciting novels by each author.

Climb aboard the Harlequin Omnibus now! The coupon below is provided for your convenience in ordering.

Violet Winspear

Omnibus

"To be able to reproduce the warmly exciting world of romance . . . a colourful means of escape", this was the ambition of the young VIOLET WINSPEAR, now a world famous author. Here, we offer three moving stories in which she has well and truly achieved this.

. . . . CONTAINING

PALACE OF THE PEACOCKS . . . where we join young Temple Lane, in the ridiculous predicament of masquerading as a youth on an old tub of a steamer, somewhere in the Java Seas. She had saved for five years to join her fiancee in this exotic world of blue skies and peacock waters — and now . . . she must escape him . . . (#1318).

BELOVED TYRANT . . . takes us to Monterey, where high mountainous country is alive with scents and bird-song above the dark blue surge of the Pacific Ocean. Here, we meet Lyn Gilmore, Governess at the Hacienda Rosa, where she falls victim to the tyrany of the ruthless, savagely handsome, Rick Corderas . . . (#1032).

COURT OF THE VEILS . . . is set in a lush plantation on the edge of the Sahara Desert, where Roslyn Brant faces great emotional conflict, for not only has she lost all recollection of her fiancee and her past, but the ruthless Duane Hunter refuses to believe that she ever was engaged to marry his handsome cousin . . . (#1267).

$1.50 per volume

Isobel Chace

Omnibus

A writer of romance is a weaver of dreams. This is true of ISOBEL CHACE, and her many thousands of ardent readers can attest to this. All of her eagerly anticipated works are so carefully spun, blending the mystery and the beauty of love.

. . . . CONTAINING

A HANDFUL OF SILVER . . . set in the exciting city of Rio de Janeiro, with its endless beaches and tall skyscraper hotels, and where a battle of wits is being waged between Madeleine Delahaye, Pilar Fernandez the lovely but jealous fiancee of her childhood friend, and her handsome, treacherous cousin — the strange Luis da Maestro . . . (#1306).

THE SAFFRON SKY . . . takes us to a tiny village skirting the exotic Bangkok, Siam, bathed constantly in glorious sunshine, where at night the sky changes to an enchanting saffron colour. The small nervous Myfanwy Jones realizes her most cherished dream, adventure and romance in a far off land. In Siam, two handsome men are determined to marry her — but, they both have the same mysterious reason . . . (#1250).

THE DAMASK ROSE . . . in Damascus, the original Garden of Eden, we are drenched in the heady atmosphere of exotic perfumes, when Vickie Tremaine flies from London to work for Perfumes of Damascus and meets Adam Templeton, fiancee of the young rebellious Miriam, and alas as the weeks pass, Vickie only becomes more attracted to this your Englishman with the steel-like personality . . . (#1334).

$1.50 per volume

Joyce Dingwell
Omnibus

JOYCE DINGWELL'S lighthearted style of writing and her delightful characters are well loved by a great many readers all over the world. An author with the unusual combination of compassion and vitality which she generously shares with the reader, in all of her books.

. . . . CONTAINING

THE FEEL OF SILK . . . Faith Blake, a young Australian nurse becomes stranded in the Orient and is very kindly offered the position of nursing the young niece of the Marques Jacinto de Velira. But, as Faith and a young doctor become closer together, the Marques begins to take an unusual interest in Faith's private life . . . (#1342).

A TASTE FOR LOVE . . . here we join Gina Lake, at Bancroft Bequest, a remote children's home at Orange Hills, Australia, just as she is nearing the end of what has been a very long "engagement" to Tony Mallory, who seems in no hurry to marry. The new superintendent, Miles Fairland however, feels quite differently as Gina is about to discover . . . (#1229).

WILL YOU SURRENDER . . . at Galdang Academy for boys, "The College By The Sea", perched on the cliff edge of an Australian headland, young Gerry Prosset faces grave disappointment when her father is passed over and young Damien Manning becomes the new Headmaster. Here we learn of her bitter resentment toward this young man — and moreso. the woman who comes to visit him . . . (#1179).

$1.50 per volume

Susan Barrie

Omnibus

The charming, unmistakable works of SUSAN BARRIE, one of the top romance authors, have won her a reward of endless readers who take the greatest of pleasure from her inspiring stories, always told with the most enchanting locations.

. . . . CONTAINING

MARRY A STRANGER . . . Doctor Martin Guelder sought only a housekeeper and hostess for his home, Fountains Court, in the village of Herford-shire in the beautiful English countryside. Young Stacey Brent accepts his proposal, but soon finds herself falling deeply in love with him — and she cannot let him know . . . (#1043).

THE MARRIAGE WHEEL . . . at Farthing Hall, a delightful old home nestled in the quiet country-side of Gloucestershire, we meet Frederica Wells, chauffeur to Lady Allerdale. In need of more financial security, Frederica takes a second post, to work for Mr. Humphrey Lestrode, an exacting and shrewd businessman. Almost immediately — she regrets it . . . (#1311).

ROSE IN THE BUD . . . Venice, city of romantic palaces, glimmering lanterns and a thousand waterways. In the midst of all this beauty, Catherine Brown is in search of the truth about the mysterious disappearance of her step-sister. Her only clue is a portrait of the girl, which she finds in the studio of the irresistably attractive Edouard Moroc — could it be that he knows of her whereabouts? . . . (#1168).

$1.50 per volume